NIGHT STALKER

The Indian watched. It was none of his business what white men would do to other white men and women, but he waited. He looked over the remains of two prairie wagons with the hope of something to give his squaw. She had recently lost her firstborn baby and her heart was heavy. He watched the two men leave and then went to inspect the dead bodies. Then he heard the wail of a baby. He had found the perfect gift for Blue Cloud . . . or so he thought.

TEX LARRIGAN

NIGHT STALKER

Complete and Unabridged

LINFORD
Leicester

First published in Great Britain in 1997 by
Robert Hale Limited
London

First Linford Edition
published 1998
by arrangement with
Robert Hale Limited
London

British Library CIP Data

Larrigan, Tex
    Night stalker.—Large print ed.—
Linford western library
1. Western stories
2. Large type books
I. Title
823.9'14 [F]

ISBN 0–7089–5277–1

Published by
F. A. Thorpe (Publishing) Ltd.
Anstey, Leicestershire

Set by Words & Graphics Ltd.
Anstey, Leicestershire
Printed and bound in Great Britain by
T. J. International Ltd., Padstow, Cornwall

This book is printed on acid-free paper

Prologue

THE Indian crouched low, watching the scene unfolding far down below in the rocky basin that was known as Apache Pass. The setting sun turned his skin to bronze. He was dressed for a hunting trip and that day had been successful. He had meat cached to last his family for several days, which was a satisfaction for his squaw had borne a child and lost it and she needed good food to recover her strength.

But now the day was shadowed by the events below. Grey Wolf was a superstitious man and it augured badly that he should see murder done by white man to white man.

He couldn't understand the logic of the white men preying upon each other. To fight an enemy of another tribe for the sake of hunting grounds was something understandable. But to kill for the pleasure of killing, and to rape another man's woman as a way of torturing her before killing her was something he reckoned was demonic.

He watched inscrutably. It didn't occur to him to stop the carnage. It wasn't his business. He could wait and then go down and examine what was left in the two wagons.

The two men below were drunk and oblivious to the eyes watching them. They yelled and laughed and drank from the whiskey bottles found in one of the wagons. One opened a chest and tossed out women's clothing in a search for money or valuables. There were papers scattered along with several stiff-backed photos of men and women sitting and standing to attention. These they ignored. It was cash, jewels and whiskey they were looking for. They ignored the bodies lying in grotesque attitudes, all shot, the men mercifully before they'd known they were ambushed.

The women . . . Grey Wolf's eyes slid over them, their nakedness disturbing. He thought of his own woman, Blue Cloud. He would follow the man who did that to her to Hell and back and then slow roast him . . .

He studied the two men. He would know them again. One had a limp and a twisted mouth. The other had bright red hair and he lacked a left hand. Oh, yes, he would know them again . . .

At last they rode away, swaying in their saddles and whooping as if they'd fought and won a major victory. Grey Wolf's lips curled in contempt. White trash. They were lower than snakes.

He clambered down below and cautiously approached the wagons. One of the horses had been shot dead, another writhed in agony in the traces and Grey Wolf cut its throat. The other two horses were still standing close up to a boulder of rock where the wagon had slewed when the driver was shot. He still hung there half on and half out of his box seat. The horses moved nervously, scenting the smell of death. Grey Wolf cut them loose. They wouldn't go far. Both were bleeding but not badly. He caught the reins and hobbled them. They would be useful back at the lodge. Horses were worth more than gold.

He looked about him for something Blue Cloud might value. He found a blackened frypan and a kettle. She would like such things. Then he heard a sound and he froze in his tracks. It was like the mewling of a kitten and a very bad-tempered kitten at that and it was growing stronger by the minute. Then it dawned on him what it was. It was a baby and a hungry one by the howls that were now filling the air around him.

It took some time to find him. The mother had been quick witted. The child was hidden in a crevice of rock hidden by the wagon. She must have slipped through the canvas and deposited the wrapped-up sleeping bundle and then gone back to help

4

defend her husband. Or maybe she'd run from the wagon to distract the men away from the baby. Her body was lying well away from the wagon and she was the mother. The other woman was a much older person.

Grey Wolf gathered up the baby and looked at it. It was red-faced and angry and gnawing its knuckles. He saw it was healthy and well-cared for with black curly hair and bright blue eyes.

Then he smiled. It had not been a bad omen after all. The Great Spirit had heard Blue Cloud's cries. These white folks had gone to their home in the sky because it was their time to go. The child had to remain and it was Blue Cloud's destiny to care for and rear it. He would call him Spirit Gift and take him home to Blue Cloud. She had milk waiting for him.

It was the best day's hunting he'd ever done.

Blue Cloud would be pleased and she would allow him into her bed again . . .

1

THE fasting and the ordeal by fire were over. Now came the last stage of the initiation, the tracking down and killing of a deer before the fast was broken.

The seven young men of the tribe who were now old enough to become men in their own right of bravery and prowess, were already weakened with their week's ordeal. Spirit Gift looked at his two friends, Little Otter and Swift Arrow and saw that they were both distressed and Little Otter was blistered and bleeding badly from the ordeal by fire.

"Take heart, Little Otter. I shall help you when we go into the forest," he whispered. Little Otter roused himself.

"No! You would undermine my courage. If I pass that test I want it to be on my terms!"

"But no one will know."

"I would know and you would know. Don't worry. I shall come through. You wait and see."

Spirit Gift sighed. Sometimes he couldn't understand his friends. They were so proud about things for which he couldn't raise any enthusiasm. His father reckoned it was because of his white blood. White men did not think or act like true men of spirit. They had a lot to learn.

He sighed again. Why couldn't he have had good Indian parents instead of being found in a bundle nearly under the wheels of a white man's wagon?

He fingered the bulky amulet he wore hanging from a strip of rawhide around his neck. He hoped the white man's god would help during this last test of ingenuity and skill. He remembered all the lessons in tracking he'd had from Grey Wolf, who was the best tracker in this band of Chiricahua Apache. Spirit Gift loved and revered him. He had been a good father and taught him all his skills of hunting, shooting with a bow as well as with a white man's rifle. He'd taught him to survive in the forest and know where the edible roots grew. He could live even in winter on his own resources if he must, and he was not afraid to be alone for the Great Spirit would always be with him, in the water, the great rocks, the boulders and the earth. Everything was supportive. He only had to trust. All would be provided.

So now why was he anxious about the outcome of this last test? He had hunted the wild beasts of the forest and killed many times before, but this time was different. He had had no food in his belly for five days and would not eat again until he returned with a carcass over his shoulders and he would not be allowed to cut out the liver and assuage the pangs of hunger gnawing his vitals. He had to prove his stamina as he would have to do so during a great famine. He had to show he was a man and could endure.

He closed his eyes and prayed. It would be doubly hard for him if he failed. He already had enemies amongst the youth of the Chiricahua Apache and they would laugh and jeer and call him dirty white trash. He would rather die than fail!

Mangus Colorado, the great overall chief was presiding over this last test. He was looking for braves to fill the gaps left by the latest battle with the US cavalry. Cochise, Mangus Colorado's son-in-law, had persuaded the old man that the new Butterfield Overland Express service was a new sign of encroachment into their territory and should be stopped. So the angered chief had made a series of raids on the coaches which were accompanied by the US military and there had been many casualties on both sides. Now the best warriors would be chosen to go with Mangus Colorado on his next raid. Rumour was that the experienced braves were in short supply and that was why these young boys were being recruited for they would taste their first blood in fighting the hated white men.

Spirit Gift was excited. Maybe he would be one of those chosen if he fared well. He touched his amulet as he waited for Mangus Colorado to blow the cow horn to signal the start of the chase.

He knew exactly where he was heading. Up into the blue mountains to the south of the great Arizona desert. They could take no rifle. They had to use a bow and arrows and were allowed a knife. They were stripped and barefoot and only the deerskin apron covered their thighs back and front. A sweatband around the head and his amulet was his only clothing. He was ready.

Then when the horn blew its mournful sound, he no longer thought of Little Otter and Swift Arrow but taking a deep breath started to run. His legs felt like jelly, his belly ached but the more he hurt, the more determined he became.

The burns on his body troubled him but he did what his father had advised when facing the fire ordeal and hypnotized himself against the pain. He was now running smoothly and rhythmically and his mind was in a space above his head, watching his body move with a certain detachment.

He headed away from the other youths who were coming behind at various paces, some beaten before they started. Soon he was far ahead and making for the terrain he knew so well.

The sun was going down. Soon it would be night and he would have to hunt in the dark, by smell and intuition as well as by ear. He knew he could do it, if he could overcome his physical self.

He *must* do it! He must find an animal before tomorrow night at sunset. Any animal would do but the larger the animal, the more prestige. He wanted to find a lordly stag and bring him home in triumph.

But there would have to be the preparation before he killed it. He would have to cleanse himself and pray to the soul of the animal and explain why he must take his life so that the soul of the animal would agree to give up its body. He must thank it so that it may go on its way to the happy hunting ground up in the sky. That way he would do no harm to the beast.

The moon was coming up when Spirit Gift reached the foothills. Now he was cautious and not running headlong, as swift as any deer. He took great breaths to conserve his energy and all the while his ears and nose were working overtime.

There were rustlings of birds as he sent out mind feelers in the forest around him. His nerves and senses were working full stretch.

Then he sniffed what he was seeking, that pungent sweaty animal scent of a beast that had been running. He stopped and lay down and listened and in the far distance he heard the unmistakable sounds of a small herd grazing somewhere ahead. He could see them in his mind's eye, some grazing and others settling for the night. The cows and calves clustered together and the stags and young males, heaving and drifting all around them in uneasy awareness of danger that might occur.

He was in luck.

Now all he had to do was cleanse himself. Make ready and then go quietly and cautiously and follow them until daybreak and choose his kill. It would be easy.

But it wasn't. Far from it. There were other hunters out that night. Not young boys, proving that they were hunting, but professional killers and they were not out to kill deer. They were on the prowl for more important prey and when Spirit Gift came upon them they had already found what they were looking for.

14

He moved forward like a cat, putting one foot down slowly and feeling for twigs that might crack before putting his weight on them. Then he paused and waited before moving again. Grey Wolf had taught him patience. He could stalk all night if he had to.

Gradually he moved around the small encampment and watched the men who sat around a small sheltered fire that threw very little light. He saw they were using the old Indian trick of shielding their flames with stones and sods of earth. These men were men of the wilderness. He had heard Grey Wolf curse such men who came and plundered and took and gave nothing back to the land.

Then as he watched he saw to his amazement that there were three prisoners lying in the shadows, bound and gagged and one of them looked like a woman.

He now had a problem. Should he quietly leave this place and go seek his herd of deer, or stay and help these prisoners? That they were white, there was no mistake. He looked at the sky and where the moon had sailed. He had plenty of time.

He considered. Yes, he could wait. So he took up a position not far from the prisoners and squatted on his haunches. He could rest and go through his cleansing ritual and wait developments. If the men slept, he could even cut the bonds free of the prisoners and then it would have to be up to them what they did.

He closed his eyes but kept his senses alert. He prayed to the beast he was to kill and asked forgiveness for the act and did all the ritual he'd been taught from a child and at the end of it, felt ready for whatever might happen.

The moon had sailed far over the sky when he thought the time was right to act. He bellied through the undergrowth and watched and waited and saw that the man on guard had dropped off to sleep with an empty whiskey bottle near his hand. Spirit

Gift's lips curled. Stupid careless fool! Grey Wolf would kill a brave who acted in such a fashion!

Carefully, he put a hand across the young girl's mouth. Her eyes flashed open in panic but he shook his head and she drew a long ragged breath as he released his hold. He sawed her wrist thongs and then the bindings around her ankles. Then putting a finger to his lips, she watched him fascinated as he freed the two men who were now awake and watching him with interest.

"Thank you," whispered the older man but Spirit Gift lifted a wary hand and he subsided but watched Spirit Gift with bright suspicious eyes. "Why?" he whispered, but again Spirit Gift shook his head and loosed the younger man. He saw they both wore the uniforms of the US soldiers.

Then without another word, Spirit Gift turned away and left the three prisoners free. He hadn't gone far before he heard shooting. He hoped they still lived, especially the young girl who was very pretty in a different sort of way to the girls in his village. He hesitated. Should he return? Then he shrugged his shoulders. Perhaps it was a test from the Great Spirit, to turn him from his path of duty. He must capture and kill the beast whose life he had prayed for. It would be waiting.

It was.

He catfooted through the undergrowth upwind of the small herd he heard in the distance. All was quiet. It was the Great Spirit's time just before dawn when all the world belonged to Him.

He saw the deer quietly grazing. It was a young bull not yet old enough to challenge for leadership. Spirit Gift let out a sigh and reached for an arrow. He was in no doubt the young stag had come to meet him.

The young bull lifted his head and looked up as he fitted his arrow to the bow. The animal stood still, calmly waiting. It knew. There was no shadow of doubt. He was ready to die.

Spirit Gift shot him cleanly in the throat. The beast threw up his head and collapsed to his knees. He lifted his head once to look at Spirit Gift and then he keeled over and was still.

Spirit Gift exulted. It had only taken one arrow! Mangus Colorado would acknowledge him as an up and coming warrior! The tribe would see, and he would be able to have the pick of the squaws . . . if he wanted them.

He frowned. He wasn't quite sure about the girls. When he thought of them, he knew instinctively that he was different. At those times he wasn't sure of himself any more.

He shrugged off the thought and concentrated on the dead stag. He was becoming increasingly weak from both hunger and thirst and this last mighty effort to complete the ritual to earn the right to be considered a man and a warrior.

He sat crosslegged and intoned the litany for the departing beast spirit and wished it well. Refreshed, he took upon his shoulders the still warm beast at a jogtrot to the village.

There, he found the whole village waiting. He wasn't the first to return but he had brought in the biggest animal. He stood, swaying a little with fatigue and Mangus Colorado stepped forward to examine the beast. He smiled.

"You have done well, son of Grey Wolf. From now on you will be known as Night Stalker. Does that please you?"

The boy known as Spirit Gift was no more. He was a man with a man's name. His heart swelled with pride.

"It pleases me very much and I am ready to follow you whenever I am needed. I swear it!"

"Good! It might be sooner than you think!"

2

THAT night, bursting with pride at his son's success and being named by Mangus Colorado himself, Grey Wolf told him about what he'd seen on that fateful day when he had saved the boy's life.

"So you see, you were a gift from the Great Spirit to me to give to Blue Cloud in her blackest hour."

Night Stalker nodded gravely. "She is a good mother." He reached over and patted her on the shoulder. She caught his hand and kissed it.

"You are a good son." She sat back, her fingers busy sewing beads on a ceremonial jerkin for him to use on special occasions. She hoped it would be for his marriage. It was made from the finest deerskin, chewed by her until it was as soft as a baby's skin.

"Tell me again about the men,

Father," Night Stalker asked quietly.

"As I said, they had ambushed the wagons in the pass. The two men must have been killed before they were aware of the ambush. The women . . . " He hesitated. "They had been raped and tortured before dying. One was your mother. The other was an older woman. There was also a young boy, maybe as old as you, a fresh-faced youth just beginning to shave. He had been tortured and killed."

Night Stalker moved impatiently. "But the men who did this?"

"Ah, yes, the men. One was redfaced with a full beard. Tall and broad and lacking a left hand. There was some kind of a hook on the end of it. The other was shorter with black hair. He looked like a mongrel dog, neither white or red. He had a twisted mouth, like one struck by the Great Spirit himself. He also had a limp like a man partially paralyzed. You understand?"

Night Stalker nodded.

"An old man's affliction. I wonder if he is still alive?"

Grey Wolf looked at him speculatively. "Why do you wonder?"

"Because I should like to meet him one day, and the other man."

Grey Wolf nodded. "I thought your reaction would be so. It is good to avenge the death of one's natural parents. It is only right and proper. We have done our best to bring you up in all honour. Now that you are a man we must allow you to take up your destiny. Whatever you decide to do will have our support." He glanced at Blue Cloud who sat impassively stitching. A tear ran down her cheek but the slight nod showed she was in agreement with Grey Wolf.

"Thank you both for what you have done for me. You have my love as a son now and forever."

"You will stay with us?"

"Of course. I am committed to Mangus Colorado."

"You are not committed to him

forever. Mangus Colorado is swayed by Cochise who wants power for himself. He plays a game with the men in Washington. He is responsible for many lives being lost. I would that we could live in peace with one another. I do not want to lose you, son, on the battlefield. I would rather you joined your white relatives than die like so many of our Apache braves."

Night Stalker was shocked.

"You speak blasphemy, Father. If Mangus Colorado or Cochise heard you, you would be killed."

Grey Wolf smiled grimly. "There are many of us who think the way I do. It is time we found a way of living with the white man. More and more of them come into our country every year. We must find a peace . . . "

"Peace, Father? How can you say such a thing? This is our country . . . "

"Not so, Night Stalker. It belongs to the Great Spirit and we are only custodians. I have explained to you before. We are here on sufferance."

"But what of the old trail that has become known by the name of the man Butterfield who now runs his mail coaches with the aid of the cursed military? Now there are forts and way-stations along the trail. Soon, there will be men coming to take the land we hunt. Is that not wrong? What will happen to our hunting grounds?"

Grey Wolf shrugged.

"The land is vast. We can move our village and settle in the wilderness."

"Is that how you see us? Every few years packing up the tepees and moving on? I think Mangus Colorado is right. We should stay and fight!"

"You are young and spirited, Night Stalker. You have not the wisdom of experience. Nothing will stop the flood of white settlers. To survive we must compromise!"

"This is all wrong," Night Stalker protested. "We should protect our rights!"

Grey Wolf shook his head slowly.

"Stop rattling spears, my son. It is

better to live than face the big guns of the army. We shall not win in the end, but lose the bravest and best young men of our tribe. Do we want that?"

Night Stalker's nostrils curled. At that moment he was all Apache. It infuriated him that his father could talk in this way. He knew he was no coward. He had heard tales all his life about Grey Wolf's prowess in battle. He had seen the scars he carried from various campaigns. So why now speak of compromise?

"I don't understand you, Father."

"You will someday when you have a grown son of your own. I only want what is best for you and the other young men of our tribe. Don't you understand that if the young life-blood of the tribe is lost, then the tribe itself is lost?"

"But you were always ready to fight!"

"Yes, but the circumstances were different. When I was young we fought the Comanche and the Sioux because of land differences and hunting grounds.

Now we face the evergrowing legions of the white men sent from Washington to take over the land. They are just the beginning of a great tidal wave that will engulf us. You will see."

"But Father . . . "

Grey Wolf held up his hand. "Enough! You have done well this last week but you must not let your coming of age go to your head! You will now sleep and recover your strength. You will need it in the days to come."

The time came sooner than he expected. Mangus Colorado sent out his runners and one came at midnight and entered the tepee of the chief. Soon, Grey Wolf and Night Stalker were summoned to Chief Hunting Bear's lodge.

Chief Hunting Bear faced them grimly.

"The war drums are beating. Mangus Colorado requires the help from our best warriors." He glanced meaningfully at Night Stalker and then at Grey Wolf. "I know how you feel about Mangus

Colorado. Is it your wish that the boy goes into battle? After all, he is not Apache . . . "

"I am Apache!" Night Stalker interrupted impetuously. "I am loyal just as if I was the real son of Grey Wolf. I regard him as my true father! It could not be otherwise. He saved my life after losing my parents to white men! I hate all white men! I always shall!" His blue eyes stared fiercely from one to another. "Please believe me. I am truly Apache."

Chief Hunting Bear nodded approvingly. He liked this boy. He'd watched him grow up from a baby and he'd always taken part in all the games designed to bring out the courage and boldness of the growing youths. He would make a good warrior when he acquired both experience and wisdom. Now he was just a hotheaded youth, who spoke as he felt. He did not yet realize the pull of blood. The chief glanced meaningly at Grey Wolf.

"You do not want him to go and

fight the white men?"

Grey Wolf considered. "I do not challenge the boy's ability, but it does not seem right. If the Comanche was our enemy, then I would be proud to send my son into battle. But against the white men in the circumstances I think it would bring bad fortune. I have a feeling in my bones."

"Then the boy will not go. You will go in his place! I have so decreed."

"But, Chief . . . " Night Stalker began to protest.

"Enough! Grey Wolf goes in your place. I have spoken," and he waved them both from the tepee.

Outside, Night Stalker balled his fists.

"I should go. You should be here for Blue Cloud."

The swing to the jaw caught Night Stalker by surprise. He stumbled and fell and lay looking up at Grey Wolf in incredulous belief.

"You struck me!" He couldn't believe it.

"You act like a child so you are punished as a child. You will obey the Chief and you will protect Blue Cloud and hunt for food and bring wood for her fire. In short, you will do a man's work. Understand?"

Night Stalker nodded. "I understand."

"Good. I can go with Mangus Colorado in good heart knowing you are looking after your mother."

He turned away leaving Night Stalker on the ground and when he returned to their tepee he was already gone. Blue Cloud was lamenting noisily.

"He will not come back! He says he had bad feelings about following Mangus Colorado! He would not listen!"

"Just where are they headed? Where is Mangus Colorado?"

"Somewhere along the trail called the Butterfield trail. There is a wagon-train heading towards Fort Dawson. It is said to be a military train carrying foodstuffs for the fort. There will be much plunder. Oh, I could wish that man in hell! We don't need another clash with the military, but Grey Wolf said he was in honour to go! It is because of you, Night Stalker! He has taken your place!"

Never before had Night Stalker heard such bitterness in her voice towards him. He felt anger and guilt. He had so wanted to go. It wasn't fair!

"I can still go and Grey Wolf can return."

"No! You will do as you are told or Grey Wolf will beat me."

"Very well. What shall I do for you today?"

"Collect firewood. I must cook the meat you brought yesterday and preserve some of it. The rest will be given to the other women who have lost their men. Now go to it and while you do so, talk to the spirit of the forest and cleanse your heart."

Night Stalker filled a pouch with food and, without a word, left the village. It would take some time to commune with the spirits as Blue Cloud wished and find enough wood to roast the young stag which by the time he returned would be skinned and ready to be put on the spit.

He trotted away vaguely aware of a vibration on the air which became more distinct as he travelled south. He knew he was running parallel with the old trail. His heart beat faster. The vibration was coming from Mangus Colorado's mighty wardrum. Maybe he would come up behind those who were gathering under the old chief's banner.

He must make his peace with the spirits first. Heart anger was a sin and he was superstitious enough to heed Blue Cloud's warning. He selected a tree and sat down crosslegged and prepared himself for meditation. He would make it quick and then he might just happen amongst the warriors and perhaps see some action.

★ ★ ★

Grey Wolf's bad feelings came back when he and the other warriors positioned themselves on the high-rising cliffs on each side of the trail which was now passing through what the Indians called Sweetwater Valley. It was a perfect place for ambush. Many a wagon-train had been destroyed in that region. It was a place of ghosts and crosses. Grey Wolf shivered.

He could see the long winding column, much larger than Mangus Colorado's runner had described. And with it were at least two platoons of soldiers. So it must be a very important train indeed.

He reckoned there was a mustering of at least 500 Indians from the small local tribes. They would have been formidable if they'd been all seasoned fighters, but half of them were inexperienced youths. Grey Wolf felt a growing anger against Mangus Colorado and his son-in-law, Cochise. Power mad they were, with no idea of saving life. They were stiff with pride, but not using their own warriors but gambling with the life-blood of the lesser tribes. He wanted to turn and run.

Then the great horror came.

Cochise waved his lance forward and the first wave of seasoned warriors bounded down the cliffs, yelling and shooting and suddenly the first four wagons were stripped of their tarpaulins as the cavalry soldiers returned fire, and instead of bales and boxes, there were four Gatling guns mounted and ready to fire, two facing south and two to the north.

The short sharp bursts of gunfire caught the Indians on both sides and, what was worse, the second wave of youths were caught in the blast and the rocks ran red with blood. Grey Wolf's bad feeling caught up with him. He thought of Night Stalker and gave thanks that he was not here with him and then he was catapulted into a great enveloping darkness . . .

The skirmish didn't last long. Mangus

Colorado and Cochise stood on a great pinnacle together and watched the disaster and along with the remaining braves disappeared into the hills, knowing a trap had been laid and been successful. It would be a long time before the Apache would respond to another call.

Down below in the confusion created by the Indian attack and the answering guns, Colonel Willoughby Jones and his sergeant regrouped his troop. Major Tad Parker was to carry on with the wagon-train and the colonel and his men would go after the fleeing Indians back to the nearest village.

They were full of glee at the ruse that had been played on Mangus Colorado and the colonel's exploits would be recounted over many campfires. The men who rode with Colonel Jones were in the throes of bloodlust and it was blood they were determined to spill.

So it was when Night Stalker was approaching the village he became aware of shots and screams and dropping his enormous load of wood, he ran to a jumble of rocks and climbing and sliding, came to the top and watched the scene below, his guts twisting and turning and making him weak.

He saw the fleeing women and children fling up their arms and drop in their tracks. He saw old men ridden down and trampled by horses. He saw his father's older brother shooting with an old army rifle and then be overpowered while he fought madly to escape. He was lashed with rope and dragged tied to a soldier's pommel until every bit of skin was scraped from his body. He looked like a skinned beast.

Then he saw Blue Cloud dragged naked from her tepee by a soldier wearing the stripes of a sergeant. She fought him madly, raking her fingernails down his cheeks, her long hair wrapped about them both.

Fury overcame discretion and Night Stalker bounded down the rocks, knife in hand and yelling the traditional Apache warcry.

He lashed out at the soldier but he was too late. The sergeant stove in Blue Cloud's head with his rifle butt, blood dripping from his cheek. Then he was knocked back by the impetus of Night Stalker's charge as the boy straddled him to plunge his knife into his breast.

The man heaved himself upwards and the boy flew through the air. He turned like a snake and headbutted the man in the stomach. The man grunted and suddenly Night Stalker was in the grasp of a tall powerful officer.

"Not so fast, young feller. We want you alive. Jenkins, stop groaning and tie this one up, and then round up any other males you find. We want the chief."

"Yes sir!" Though Night Stalker struggled, he was trussed up like a prairie chicken. Then he was dragged to the middle of what once had been the main meeting ground. There was no sign of Chief Hunting Bear, only several old men and boys.

Then, fastened with ropes to the pommels of the cavalry horses, they trotted or were dragged as booty back to the fort.

Night Stalker scarcely noticed his torment. He had withdrawn into himself, his earlier training for his coming of age ordeal standing him in good stead. He cried inwardly for Blue Cloud and vowed to himself that some day he would kill the man the officer called Jenkins . . .

3

JOE ADAMS looked down from the office window into the busy square in the heart of San Francisco. There was much activity going on down there, for one of the Butterfield stagecoaches had just driven in with much shouting and cracking of whips to announce its arrival.

It was a feat of endurance for the mailcoach to come the 2,600 miles from Tipton, Missouri to San Francisco. It had taken twenty-four days and they had changed horses at 139 way-stations, picking up and setting down passengers *en route*. Two drivers and a guard made up the crew and they were all seasoned Indian-fighters for one never knew when a petty uprising might take place.

Joe Adams always experienced that aching nostalgia whenever the stage came in. He remembered the time when he was a boy and listened to the tales around the camp-fire of attacking wagon-trains and lone stagecoaches. Then, it had seemed the right thing to do. White men were the hated enemy. Now, he was all white with but a fading memory of freedom in the wilderness.

He thought back to the day he was captured and dragged back to Fort Dawson and into the presence of Colonel Willoughby Jones and Major Tad Parker.

He was being interrogated and he sullen and mute stared defiantly at the man with the stripes called Jenkins who had the effrontery to think he could break him by merely lashing his back with a bullwhip. He stood proud, away inside himself as his father had instructed him before the coming of age ritual, and the pain was far away and not part of him.

Suddenly his concentration had wavered and died and the pain came swooshing back for the major had stepped forward and bellowed the words which saved his life.

"Stop! This is the boy who saved my life and my daughter's. He is the one I told you about who came and loosed our bonds and then disappeared into the darkness. I never even thanked him." Major Tad Parker was just in time to catch the boy known as Night Stalker as he collapsed.

After that, Joe Adams could never remember fully what happened next, but he awakened one morning on an uncomfortably soft bed wrapped in a strange smelling quilt and a young girl was trying to feed him soup and it was dribbling all down his front.

He'd glared at her and she'd run away and after awhile the major and his wife had come to talk to him.

He'd known little of the white man's language and so it had been miming with a sprinkling of English and Apache words but somehow he'd understood what was required of him.

It took time to realize he was not

41

in danger and most of that time was spent with Annie Parker, who had taught him English, and in doing so, house-trained him. He smiled now as he thought back over the last ten years, Annie had done so much for him.

He appreciated her bravery in coping with him, for looking back, he could see that he had been a wild animal of a boy, with his back to the wall like a rat in a corner and it was she who'd come to understand him and tame him. He loved her. He would give his life for her.

He watched as the passengers stepped down from the coach, stiff and weary. Two were city men in dark store clothes and one looked like a flamboyant gambler. The other passenger was a woman and a mighty fine woman too! She made his heart quicken.

He watched the padlocked mailbox being dumped on to the ground by the two drivers. It would be heaved into the ground-floor office of the

Butterfield Overland Mail Carriers to be signed for and then delivered to the government mail delivery office. There would also be strongboxes destined for the local Bank. He had watched the same scene many times before.

He left the window and the room and prepared to take charge of the boxes prior to delivery. The drivers greeted him cheerfully and the elder held out his hand.

"Hi, Joe! Back in one piece as usual." They clasped hands and Ned Mullaney grinned. "We knocked two days off. I hope your old man is honouring that bonus he offered?"

"Sure. George Adams's word is his bond. Surely you know that, you old cuss! I'll see you and Jake get it. I promise!"

"We'd better. It was those Apache friends of yours who made the wheels roll! They sure are persistent sonsofbitches! Rode with us nigh on fifty miles before we shook 'em off. Lucky for us, a detail out of Fort

Fitzwilliam happened along and scared the devils away."

"Not scared, Ned, just realistic. They live to fight another day. You never describe Apaches as scared. Remember that, Ned."

"Sorry, Joe, I wasn't thinking."

Joe smiled. "No offence taken, Ned."

He turned away and devoted himself to the bestowal of the boxes. Ned watched him curiously. Joe wasn't only an Indian lover, he *was* an Indian despite being of white blood. The older man felt pity for this young man who was neither one or the other.

Later, Joe had time to think of the Apache skirmish. He wondered who was chief warmonger these days. He had only been back once to the dreary site that had been his home village. It was nothing but a scar on the landscape, a charred overgrown mass of scrub where tepees had once stood. He'd seen the communal grave where those who had died that fateful day were buried. Once more Joe had made vow to find the man Jenkins and kill him.

That vow was what made him restless now. Time was passing and since he, Joe had left the good major and his family he had lost touch with the regiment and with Sergeant Jenkins.

It had been Annie Parker who'd given him back his home. When he could read and write, she'd teased him to open the package he insisted on wearing around his neck and they had both pored over the sepia-coloured pasteboards and then she had read out loud the words on the sheets of paper written in small neat writing.

It was then he found out that he was Joseph Adams, son of John and Lucy Adams and they and Lucy's parents, William and Martha Jarvis were on their way to San Francisco to join John Adams's father who had financed an overland express in a partnership with an experienced stagecoach driver called John Butterfield.

It hadn't taken long for Major Parker to contact George Adams and give him the news he had a grandson of about fifteen years of age. The rest was history. A year after he was captured he was transported to San Francisco and he lost touch with Major Parker and the pretty girl called Annie.

He thought of them often, especially when he thought of Jenkins. Slow rage burned within him. He knew that some day there would be a confrontation and the sleeping cougar that was in him would raise its head and growl deep in its throat.

He knew also, that under the conventional garb of George Adams's grandson, there still lurked the Indian known as Night Stalker.

The strongboxes from the mailcoach were now all signed for and delivered and Joe Adams sat at his desk checking bills of lading for the next long journey back to Missouri along with the passengers who would join the coach as it journeyed along the route, passing the next incoming coach somewhere on the way.

It was a lucrative enterprise which gave George Adams a good return on his money, and John Butterfield his independence, thanks to Joe looking after the San Francisco office, to go and arrange new routes to add to the network.

But old George didn't rely on the income from the interest on his money. His first stake had come way back during the gold rush and from then on punching cows for Charlie Goodnight in Colorado. But George didn't believe in getting by using his own sweat. He soon realized that to grow rich, one had to use other men. So, each time he amassed a stake, he loaned his money out and grew rich on the backs of others.

The two disappointments in his life were his sons. The elder had married back East and was killed along with his wife on the way to San Francisco. He had not even known they'd had a child on the long journey. Joe was an unforeseen bonus, the reason now he lived and schemed for the boy's future.

The other deeper disappointment was his son, Zacharia, who'd gone bad. He hadn't seen him for years having bribed him to get out of the territory before the law caught up with him. He never wanted to hear the name Zach Adams again, not ever.

Now, he took his ease on his cattle ranch, some hundred miles from San Francisco. There was a rail spur coming past the ranch and he made a nice profit from cattle sent direct to the cattle yards in the city. After a lifetime of ups and downs, he was now a happy man and his only disappointment was that Joe didn't seem in a hurry to choose a girl and marry and settle down and produce some more little Adamses.

Joe looked up from his work as a shadow came between him and the light. He saw the tall, black-suited gambling man from the stage. His clothing was flamboyant, his wide-brimmed black hat studded with silver conches that must have cost a lot. His shirt was white and fancy but Joe's eyes were drawn to the twin Colts strapped low down on his hips. They looked ready for business.

"What can I do for you, sir?"

For a long moment the man stared at him up and down and Joe decided the stranger would certainly know him again. Then, "I am wanting to know the whereabouts of Mr George Adams. I understand he is a silent partner of Mr John Butterfield."

Joe put down his pen and leaned back in his chair.

"And who might be asking about him?"

The stranger frowned. "I take it you are an employee here and so it is none of your business. I just want to know where he lives in town."

"He doesn't."

"What? If he doesn't, where the hell is he? He's not dead?"

"Nope! Retired and taking it easy as he should at his age."

"Well, I'll go to hell! I've come all this way to see him. Now exactly where does he live?"

"Why should I tell you? I don't know who you are and maybe he don't want to see you!"

The stranger's eyes flashed and his long slim fingers flexed and hovered over gun butts. Joe's eyes did not waver. Gently he opened a drawer and drew out his own weapon and placed it delicately on the desk top.

"I should be mighty careful, mister. This popgun has a hair-trigger and makes a mess of a feller's chest. Now if you want to prove my words . . ." They glared at each other and then the stranger took his hands away from his gun butts.

"Now there's no need for the rough stuff, young feller. I'm family, y'know. Have you ever heard of Zach Adams? All I need to know is where my old man hangs out, is all."

Joe let out a deep breath. He certainly had heard of Zach Adams, many times when the old man was drunk. Resentment was still bitter after all the years since the banishment.

"Yes, I've heard of Zach Adams and none of it good. I don't think the old man is in any condition to take the shock of seeing you."

"Why, you young puppy! You should mind your mouth. I've shot men for less!"

"Yes? Well, do you want to try your hand?" Joe tensed. He might be sitting behind an office desk in a store suit, but he could as sure as hell grab his .45 and plug his man before the man decided to spit.

Zach Adams didn't answer. He merely walked to the door and gave a whistle and waited. Within seconds, the two business-suited men from the stage stepped inside and for the first time, Joe got a good look at them. His blood ran cold. He remembered Grey Wolf's account of how he'd found him bundled in a blanket, partially hidden between a boulder and one of the wagons of the white folk massacred by two white men.

These strangers matched the descriptions given by Grey Wolf except that they were older and the red-haired man's hair had faded to a dirty grey. But he still carried a hook where his left hand should be.

He scarcely looked at the smaller man who limped and whose mouth was twisted. Grey Wolf's eyes had been keen!

Joe's own eyes did not betray what he was thinking and he was thinking furiously. Perhaps it was best he should give old George's whereabouts and get these thugs out of town. As strangers they would have to take the old trail which wound around and about to bypass the mountainous terrain. He himself could ride over the little known Indian trail which crossed Eagle Pass and down through the Stinkwater marsh.

He could do it and be ready and waiting for these men a full day ahead of them.

He looked at all three. The crippled man smirked.

"Not so goddamned mouthy now, son! You can't take us all!"

Joe shrugged. "Why should I? I'm only doing my job."

"Now you're being sensible. So, where does my old man hang out?"

"South, down near San Antonio Falls. Anyone down there will tell you where the Adams ranch is."

"Good. Now where can I hire a coach?"

Joe looked surprised. "You need a coach?"

"Yes. My woman is travelling with us."

Joe remembered the woman and all the baggage. This visit looked as if it was meant to be permanent. He wondered what old George would make of it all. George was quick-tempered. He'd suffered himself when he hadn't seen eye to eye with the old man.

"If you go down the street to the livery stable, you'll find Sam Homer hires out an old Celerity coach, a bit battered but it will get you there."

"Good enough for a lady?"

"Yeh, if she's not too particular."

Zach Adams grunted.

"She won't have to be. Thanks for your time. See you around."

They left and Joe called for Matthew, the clerk who'd worked for the Butterfield Overland long before Joe came to San Francisco.

"I'm going to leave you in charge, Matt. Something's come up and I have to go and see the boss. There's no more coaches due for four days and maybe not then. I'll be back as soon as I can."

"But Mr Joe . . . "

"You can cope. It's serious, Matt. You know who's come to see the old man?" He paused and then said slowly, "Zach Adams. And you know what that means."

Matt whistled through his teeth. "Cor! The old man will blow his brains out as soon as he sees him!"

"Not if Zach and his buddies take him by surprise. That's why I must leave and go to him over the old Indian trail. I can be there well before Zach and I can warn him and fort up if necessary."

Matt put a gnarled fist on to Joe's shoulder.

"You've sure turned out a good kid, Joe, even if you were a wild Indian when you first came to us. You go and do what you can before all hell breaks loose! I know George. He'll kill the bastard if he had a chance and might get killed himself!"

Dawn was breaking on the third morning as Joe rode up to the final peak before picking his way down through the last pass on to Adams land locally known as the GA ranch.

Joe was dressed for travelling having exchanged store clothes for easy riding canvas jeans and deerskin jerkin with a red sweatband on his brow and wearing old scuffed boots for comfort. He rode his favourite mare. His arms were free and muscular. He looked and felt like an Indian. This was his favourite way to travel.

He checked the two guns slung low on his hips, the cartridge belt hanging crosswise from one shoulder and partially hidden by his jerkin. Hanging down his back, Indian fashion, he carried a knife, a habit from his early hunting days.

He pulled up the mare and considered the surrounding country. It was good fertile land and he could see his grandfather's herds scattered on all sides. It looked as if it had been a good year for breeding stock.

He had to give the old man credit for gathering together a loyal crew who did his bidding and kept the cattle and the boundaries in good heart.

As he looked about at the familiar landscape it came to him that this was why Zach Adams had returned. He meant to claim this land and all George's assets as being his only son and heir. Then Joe's thoughts turned to the two henchmen and he faced the facts squarely. Facts he hadn't wanted to face earlier. But now out on the silence and freedom with just the wind whistling through the trees he knew that when his grandfather saw the two men with his son, Zach, he would know who had ordered the killing of his older son.

For Joe had told the story over and over again to George as told to him by Grey Wolf and described the men well. The moment George Adams saw Zach's two buddies, he would have the answers as to why his son and daughter-in-law and her parents were slaughtered.

But the two men had slipped up. No one, not even George Adams, had known that he was a grandfather and a baby boy had been hidden away and would be found by a compassionate

Indian who would take that baby home for his wife to succour . . .

Joe smiled. They were all in for a shock. He wanted to see their faces when they realized their blunder . . . the red-haired man and his twisty-faced partner, and he wanted to witness the rage and anger when Zach Adams realized he'd had George Adams's grandson within killing range . . .

For there was no doubt in his mind. When Zach realized his brother had fathered a son, then the danger would turn on himself.

He dug his heels into the mare's ribs and she sprang forward, delighted to have her head. They went at a gallop for the last two miles and, as they came down into the valley, he saw movement around the house. The old man was still vigilant in his old age, and he would get out his spyglass and there would be hot coffee and biscuits waiting when he arrived.

He would also know that there was an

emergency. The old man was no fool. He would rap out a list of questions as he supped his coffee and ate the new-baked biscuits. His answers must be ready.

4

HIS knuckles turned white on the cane as George Adams leaned forward to listen to Joe. His piercing blue eyes, so like Joe's, sparkled in temper and disbelief.

"So he's got the gall to come here! I thought I was done with him for good!" The cane thumped the ground in temper. "He'll get no welcome here! You know why he's coming, don't you, boy? It's to see if I've got one foot in the grave! That's what! I'll see him in Hell before he inherits one foot of this land! I'll see him rot first!"

"Grandpa, calm yourself, or you'll have a heart attack!"

Joe was alarmed at the effect of Zach's name on the old man. He wondered again at the depth of the bitterness. There must be much more than the fact that Zach Adams had been a womanizer and rustler of his father's stock. It was a much deeper thing and the secret of it was eating the old man up. He sighed. He had no right to pry into the old man's affairs. Whatever had happened had done so long before he was born.

But Joe respected and admired George Adams. His word was his bond and he knew from those who worked for him that he was a fair and good boss and in his younger days would work alongside his men in any difficult task. He didn't ask of his men what he wasn't prepared to do himself.

"Grandpa, I think he aims to stay. He's bringing his woman and . . . " He paused. Should he mention the two men who were coming too? Then looking at the angry face he decided that one shock at a time was enough. "They're bringing a mountain of baggage," he finished.

"Then they can turn right round and ride back to town! I'll not even give them house-room! And not one dollar will he get out of me. He'll be broke. You can count on it. How long do we have, do you think, before they come?"

Joe shrugged. "Depends. If they get lost . . . " He grinned. "Could be days."

"He'll be here. He was always a lucky bastard. He's got the instinct of a homing pigeon."

It seemed George was right. The lumbering heavy-laden Celerity wagon lumbered into the yard two days later. George stared from his rocking-chair on the veranda at his wayward son, noting the changes in his appearance, the streaks of grey in the once black curly hair, the hard graven lines on the once round features. Zach had aged and aged badly. He looked more than his fifty odd years. George felt a glow of satisfaction. The boy had suffered wherever he had gone during the intervening years.

George's eyes narrowed as he saw

the two men helping down the woman, but his attention was again on his son who ignored what was going on behind him but came with slow strides to stand wide-legged in front of his father. Not as a prodigal son come home in humility but as some conqueror. George's hackles rose. He waited.

"Howdy, Pa. Aren't you going to welcome home your only son?"

"I have no son, and you're not welcome."

The ingratiating smile was gone. Zach scowled.

"You're in your dotage, Pa. I'm your son, Zach. Don't you know me?"

"I know you and I know what you are. Now git and take that trollop with you *and* the men you've brought to back you up! Never could do anything on your own. You always got someone else to do you dirty work!"

Zach laughed bitterly. "You always hated me, just because I was Ma's favourite."

"And you killed her! What with

63

your rampaging around and your sly disgusting habits with women, paying for your depraved pleasures with my cattle! Oh yes, you broke her heart and killed her all right!"

Zach paled.

"I'm a different man to what I was then. Believe me, Pa . . ."

"Believe you? I'd rather believe in a rattlesnake than you!"

"You need me, Pa. I'm your flesh and blood. I've got a right to come back. You're getting old and need someone of your own to care for you."

"Don't give me that bullshit. You came back to see just how things were. You'll not get your greedy hands on a foot of this land. My Will's made all nice and tight. So get that into your craw!"

"You would leave what you have to a stranger?"

"Not a stranger, boy. My grandson, Joe Adams."

"That's a lie! You have no grandson!"

"No? Well, let me surprise you, boy. Hey, Joe! Get yourself out here and introduce yourself to your Uncle Zach!"

Joe, who had been inside listening to the exchange, now came out and stood beside the old man's chair.

"Howdy again, Uncle Zach."

"*You!*" Zach laughed raucously, drawing the woman's attention. She strolled over, hips swaying and stood beside him and looked at Joe. "If I'd known who you were I'd have . . . " Zach broke off and slipped an arm about the woman. He smiled but there was anger at the back of his eyes. "Meet Tilly, folks, the best sharpshooter in the West!"

George grunted and Joe looked at her with interest. She was at least ten years older than he was and twenty years younger than Zach. She was flamboyant rather than good-looking. Her face, thickly made-up to hide old smallpox scars, was hard. She had lived fast and furiously and it showed. But she exuded sex and the low cut of her emerald-green velvet gown accentuated her calling. The green bonnet with the black feather contrasted sharply with the profusion of carefully arranged blonde curls that hung to her shoulders. She was the kind of woman a cowpuncher dreamed of during long nights out on the range.

"Howdy, Tilly," Joe managed.

Tilly smiled. "And you are?"

"Joe, miss."

"We'll have to take time out to get to know each other."

"No you won't!" George butted in. "We'll feed you and give you a bed for the night, but you're all leaving in the morning. Is that clear?"

"Now, pa . . . "

"That's it. If you don't like it, you can start back right now!" and George stumped his way inside.

Zach stared at Joe balefully. "So you're John's son. I didn't know he had a son. How come you survived the . . . er . . . massacre?"

"I was overlooked by the men sent to kill my parents. I was found and raised as an Apache."

"You were, by God? You were one lucky sonofabitch."

"I also have a description of the men who killed my father and raped my mother before she died!"

Zach started. "You have? Does the old man know this?"

"Why do you want to know? What interest is it of yours?"

Zach shrugged. "I'm your uncle. I'm interested in you. We could be friends."

Joe laughed. "My adoptive father used to speak of men who had forked tongues. I think you are one of them."

Tilly moved restlessly.

"Must you talk forever, Zach? I need the privy and then a wash and something to eat. Let's go inside while Rufus and Perce bring in the bags."

"I should leave them where they are, miss. The old man is sure a stubborn man. You'll be leaving come morning time."

She pouted. "Surely I could have a bath?"

"By all means. I'll get the housekeeper to get the tub ready. As for the men, maybe they should go straight to the bunkhouse. I'd not like Grandpa to recognize them." He turned to Zach. "You'd all best leave with no trouble, mister."

Zach frowned. "You know then?"

"Yes. It don't take much reasoning, mister."

Tilly looked from one to the other.

"What *is* this, Zach? What's all this squaring up to each other all about?"

"Never you mind. It's none of your business."

"Then I'm going inside and to hell with you!"

She shrugged and flounced off, taking her small case with her. Zach followed. Joe looked across at the watching men.

"You can bunk down with the men.

68

Willie!" he called and an old bow-legged cow-puncher poked his head out of the bunkhouse door while wiping his hands on a dirty towel.

"Yes, boss?"

"Show these men where they can bunk down and feed 'em. They'll be leaving in the morning."

He didn't wait for an answer and so missed the scowls of the two men.

Inside, he could feel the tension in the air. Tilly had already gone with the housekeeper in tow and Zach was speaking passionately to his father whose chin stuck out aggressively.

Joe recognized that look. He'd come up against it many times in the past when he'd been a wild, untamed youngster. Zach could talk until he was blue in the face. His father was hard and unforgiving. What he said was law. His word was his bond whether right or wrong and once his mind was made up, that was it. No mess.

They both turned to look at him when he entered quietly and joined them. His grandfather's eyes were coldly blue like his own. His uncle's eyes were also blue but now dark and furiously angry and spitting out an ugly message.

His own message too was clear. There was no need for words. It was as if Zach had thrown down the war lance and Joe had taken it and snapped it in half. Both knew the score. Both were on guard.

The old man broke the tension.

"Zach wants to stay and prove himself. He says I should give him one more chance. What do you say to that, Joe?"

Joe shrugged.

"It's your decision, Grandpa. He's your son. I can return to San Francisco tomorrow."

"Not so fast, boy. I haven't made up my mind. There's been too many years gone by and too much between us to make hasty decisions. I've come to live without you, Zach. I haven't had a son for years and I'm too old and goddamn

70

stubborn to change now!"

"Why, you old bastard, you've been playing with me! You've already made up your mind to toss me out! I suppose I'm disinherited too? You're hard enough for that!"

"You were disinherited the day you rode away with the contents of my safe in your saddle-bags! You've had your last dollar out of me, boy. So you're leaving in the morning, pronto. Is that clear?"

Zach didn't answer but after giving Joe a baleful glance he slammed out of the ranch-house presumably to look for his men.

"Joe," the old man said softly, "there goes trouble. What I want you to do tomorrow is to take a couple of the boys and ride the fence and check on the cattle. I have a feeling in my bones we might be in for a spot of rustling."

Joe glanced sharply at him.

"You don't mean . . . ?"

"Not Zach himself, but he has some

very dodgy friends. I can read his mind. If he can't get the dough out of me one way, he'll try another. Believe me, he's on the run and he's strapped for cash! He wouldn't be here otherwise!"

Joe left early next morning. There was no sign of the woman or his uncle or the two men with him. The ranch crew were already up and getting on with the business of the ranch. Danny Two Rivers a half-breed who was a good tracker and Big Hans Andersen, a blond giant of a Swede, a good wrangler and fast with his fists were chosen as the best men for the job on hand. They took enough grub to last three days under any conditions. They had no idea of what they might come up against. But there were two line cabins they could make for if they needed shovels or pulleys to drag cows out of crevices or swamp and there were fencing posts and wire stashed away if new fencing was to be rigged up.

The first day they saw riders way

across the plain herding a bunch of cattle. The Swede swept the area with his field-glasses.

"Some of Tad Parker's boys rounding up strays," he said laconically.

"Tad Parker? I didn't know he ranched round here?"

"Yeh. Quit the army five-six years ago. Mr Adams advised him about buying the spread. I thought you would know."

Joe thought of Annie. His heart leapt. It would be good to see her again.

"No. He never told me. I wonder why?" He felt a gust of anger against his grandfather. The old man would play God once too often.

He was quiet while they rode the fence, stopping twice to repair gaps that had been trampled down. Once they stopped to drag an old bull out of a bed of mesquite and a bellowing calf had to be reunited with its mother.

They ate at noon and rested under the shade of a jutting boulder as the sun beat down. Joe raised his hat and wiped his forehead and his sweatband with his bandanna before tipping the hat over his eyes. He slumbered, then came awake grabbing for his gun.

"What the hell's that?" Both Danny and Hans were reaching for their weapons. Danny scrambled up the incline and looked over the rim to the valley below.

"It looks mighty like a hold-up," Danny answered tersely. "Take a look, boss. There's a coach down there."

Joe scrambled to get a better view.

"Well, it's not Zach's outfit. They're going the wrong way."

Hans followed and used his glasses and his sharp intake of breath drew Joe's attention.

"What is it, Hans?"

"It's the Parker coach, boss. Tad Parker has a coach for his wife and daughter when they visit town. I've seen 'em there and it's usually loaded with women's stuff. It'll be worth the pickings, boss."

"Let's get down there pronto and sort 'em out!"

They left the horses in the shade and, checking guns, they proceeded at a fast crouch to run from cover to cover until they neared the hold-up. One horse still in the traces was down and still kicking feebly. The other stood with head down and sides heaving as if the two horses had galloped headlong before stopping.

There were two men, oblivious to the newcomers. Joe recognized them immediately. The cripple was holding a gun at a young girl's throat while an older woman lay ominously still on the ground close by. The big man with the greying red hair was busy breaking open a strongbox on the ground beside the open door of the coach, the dead driver still hanging half on and half off his box seat.

The click of three triggers drew their attention. The crippled man snapped off a shot and missed in his sudden panic. But he held on to the girl.

Danny took a slug in the arm as

he traded shots with the big man. He cursed, his arm useless. Joe took a dive for the man's legs and landed above him. The impetus rolled them over and over as both fought for supremacy. Joe, the lighter man but the more agile, at last got the man pinned down.

"Got you, you bastard. Now I want some answers." He looked around for Danny and saw him crouched low but transfixed, for the cripple had the girl in a cruel grip and his gun pointed to her temple.

Just then the man beneath him heaved his legs upwards and Joe catapulted over his head and he hit a rock. Dazed, he tried to claw himself upright and then a deep laugh stayed him in his tracks.

"I thought this little trap would bring you running! You did well, boys. I thought I was going to have to join the fun." Zach Adams, along with his woman, stepped out from behind a huge boulder, gun held loosely in his hand.

"And what do you want? You're supposed to be on your way to San Francisco."

"You, my dear nephew. You! Tie them all up, fellers and then we'll head back to Parker's ranch. We've got at least three days before the hands come heading back."

"What about Parker? What's happened to him?"

"Oh, he's being taken care of. You don't think I came all the way from 'Frisco, just to see my father?"

"Just why did you come?" Joe gritted his teeth as his hands were dragged behind his back and tied.

"To get Parker. He and I go back a long way, but that ain't any of your business. I reckon I can kill two birds with one stone by getting a hold of you."

"Zach . . ." Tilly pulled at his arm. He shrugged her off.

"Be quiet, Tilly. This is man's business."

"I didn't follow you to this godforsaken

backwoods to be an accessory to murder!"

"Cut the crap, girl. You knew the score."

"But this is your nephew, Zach. Let him go!"

"Like hell! As far as I'm concerned, he's just a renegade Indian with a white skin! He could be fooling my pa. I never knew my brother was married, never mind being a father!"

"How could you? You never kept in touch with your father!"

"That point didn't worry you until now." Zach's eyes narrowed. "You haven't taken a fancy to him, have you? You're old enough to be his mother!"

Tilly's cheeks flushed with anger. "You're a dirty rat, Zach Adams! I wish I'd never set eyes on you!"

"You'd be in jail if it wasn't for me! I could still turn you in and testify it was you who pulled the trigger and killed that gambler and not the potboy as you alleged. They'd lynch you if those jaspers back East knew you'd sent an innocent boy to the gallows!"

Tilly's face was ashen. "You wouldn't do that, Zach, after all we've meant to each other?"

"Not if you keep that big mouth shut about my business. I'm only pointing out what could happen."

Tilly looked down, her fingers twisting together.

"I'm sorry, Zach. I let my tongue run away with me."

"Right. We'll say no more about it. Now let's get this little lot back to the ranch."

Joe struggled but his bonds were too tight. The cripple, Perce, thrust his gun viciously into the girl's neck until she screamed.

"Settle yourself, mister, or this gun might go off and tell that bastard Swede of yours to back off."

"All right, Perce, I'm here now. I'm sure these folks are going to be sensible for the girl's sake. You and Rufus can go and round up their horses. They'll not be far away."

Joe ground his teeth in frustration. He wasn't near enough to Annie to give her any comfort. The girl was visibly shocked and when Perce let her go she sank down beside the body of her mother and took her in her arms ignoring the blood which welled from a wound in the head.

When the men and horses returned, she was roughly dragged from her mother and hoisted on to Zach's horse and she rode in front of him while Joe and Hans and the wounded half-breed were shackled with their own lariat. Then the little cavalcade moved at full speed towards the Parker ranch.

There, Joe was amazed to see at least a dozen men lounging in the yard as they trotted in. Some were squatting in the dust playing craps, while others played poker or just lounged with a jug of beer to hand.

They all crowded around as they came to a halt, clapping and cheering and a giant of a man with a full-length black beard lifted Annie from Zach's horse.

"Careful with her, Jonty. Don't crack her ribs with those great paws of yours!" Everyone laughed.

"So it came off then? You actually stopped the coach!" A man in a ragged blue uniform stepped onto the veranda of the ranch and looked down at them. He frowned. "Where's Missis Parker?"

Zach looked him straight in the eyes.

"She's dead, Pete. Poked her head out of the coach and caught a bullet."

"You fool! I said I wanted her alive!"

Zach flushed. "Nobody calls me a fool, Pete, not even you!"

"What you going to do about it?" snarled Pete, and suddenly there was silence amongst the men. Zach looked around at the tense faces and realized this wasn't the time to fight with Pete.

"All right . . . all right. I'll let it go this time. But I warn you be careful, buster!" He nodded to Perce and Rufus who led away the horses with Joe and his boys to the barn. Each man was shackled to a wall chain and then the door was shut.

"Well," said Hans into the darkness. "What do we do now boss?"

"Find a light and look at Danny's wound. How you feeling, Danny?"

"Stiff and sore, but I'll live. I think the bullet went right through the muscle and missed the bone."

"Good. We'll get you bandaged. I think I can reach you with one hand if you lean towards me."

With a lot of grunting and heaving, Danny got a rough bandage into place and then Joe had time to think.

But he wasn't thinking about ways to escape, he was thinking about the man, Pete. The last time he had seen him, he was Sergeant Jenkins, the man who'd beat hell out of him . . . the man he'd sworn to seek out and kill some day . . .

5

ZACH ADAMS toed the unconscious man. There was no sign of life.

"Mebbe you went too far, Jenkins. There'll be nothing but trouble if Parker's dead. We need him alive, you hotheaded fool! Get Perce to look him over. He was a doctor once. He should fix him if he can he fixed."

Jenkins looked at the still figure dispassionately.

"He had it coming to him. He was a bastard. He had me thrown into the brig for having fun with a couple of pesky Indians. Ordered me to have twenty lashes too. My back was cut to ribbons. I hope the swine dies!"

Zach Adams looked at him curiously.

"So you knew him before I asked you to join me? And you never told me?"

"Why should I! What's between us is

my business. Lost touch with him when the war was over. I always reckoned to find him some day, and you dropped him right into my hands. I want more than his cows and his dough. I want the man himself. He made me suffer. Now I make him suffer! I only wish his woman was still alive. I fancied her years ago. Still, there's the daughter. We could all have some fun with her!" His laugh bellowed forth like that of a demon from hell. Zach looked at him with distaste.

If it wasn't for the fact he needed this man and his followers to help run off the cows, he would have pulled out of the deal but suddenly it dawned on him that maybe it wasn't going to be easy getting rid of this brute. He was outnumbered.

Then there was his father to think about. He would show the old devil he wasn't going to be kicked out on his arse like one of the drifters who came by looking for a handout. He was more than a drifter. He was his father's son, goddamn!

His thoughts turned to Joe. The bloody white Indian, he'd never reckoned on. A nasty surprise, but one which could be rectified.

He watched Perce examine Parker. The rancher was black and blue and his face so swollen he didn't look like a man. Perce got up from his knees and grunted.

"Ribs stove in and suffering concussion. You want me to bind him up?"

"Yeh. Do what you can. I want him alive."

"Someone sure hates him."

"That mad dog, Jenkins. Knew him during the war. In the same regiment. The sooner we do what we planned the better and we'll get right away and hightail it back to Kansas where the pickings are easier to come by."

"What about your old man?"

"Don't worry about him. I'll fix him and you'll get your cut. The old devil's loaded and he'll pay a lot on a promise to return his precious grandson!"

85

Perce eyed him narrowly, lips curled. "You'd return him?"

"Yeh, why not? He can have the honour of burying him!"

Perce began to laugh and his thin haggard face flushed as a fit of coughing threatened to choke him.

"You all right, feller? I don't want you kicking the bucket before this little caper is over!"

"I'm fine, boss," Perce spluttered. "Just tickled that the old man would be buying a corpse. That be all."

"Well, look to Parker. Get the girl to help you. She'll do what she can for her old man. Slap her if you have to. I'm going to see what Tilly's found in the kitchen."

She was busy coaxing the fire to burn up and was cursing mightily in the doing of it. Tilly wasn't used to kitchen chores and took badly to it. She saw Zach and picked up a heavy iron pan and held it threateningly.

"If you don't get one of Jenkins's men in here to cook, I'll stove your head in! Either that or I'll poison you all with that muck that's stinking in that stewpan over there!" She pointed to a foul-smelling pan filled with something growing green mould.

"Jesus! It don't look as if Parker had a cook when the missis went to town! See what you can rustle up, Tilly, there's a good girl."

"I'm not cooking for that rattlesnake, Jenkins, or his gang. They can cook for themselves! I ain't aiming to be slave to those low-down dirty hogs! I didn't come out here to be cook, slut and bottle washer! I thought I was bettering myself. You said . . . "

"Aw, shut your mouth! I've heard it all before! Just rustle up some grub, will you?"

Tilly waggled her hips and turned, grumbling, to peer into the blackened stewpan with pursed lips. She sniffed pointedly.

"Get that girl in here. She can tell me where everything is."

"She's helping Perce with her old man."

Tilly paused, pan forgotten.

"Is he going to die?"

"He'd better not. I want him alive!"

"Why? What's special about him?"

"He's ex-military with powerful friends for one thing and for another, he's sitting on a whole heap of dough . . . in the bank, that is. I checked him out good and proper. I'll split the cows with Jenkins but we keep quiet about the cash, right?"

"You must think Jenkins a fool! He'll know how he's fixed! He's been studying Parker for years and waiting for his chance and you gave him it. You know what I think, Zach?"

"No, what do you think?"

"I think you've dropped yourself in shit, man. He's playing you for a sucker. He's laughing at you. He knows the value of that girl just as you do. He's out to break Parker and I wouldn't be surprised if he sees you and your old man as a bonus. I would

in his place. And as for that boy
. . . he's a goner and it won't be you
sending him back to his grandfather."

"You're mad! You always had a
good imagination!" But Zach looked
worried.

"Yes, and I'll tell you something else.
He'll send *you* back with that boy!"

Zach's slap knocked her back,
narrowly missing falling into the
fireplace. A ladle and a meathook
clattered on to the stone hearth. She
grabbed the meathook and lunged at
Zach and he leapt back.

"Hold it, you mad bitch! You know
damn well not to rile me! I know
what I'm doing and I'm in charge!
Pete Jenkins will do as I say. Parker's
crew won't find his cows and calves
that they've gone hunting for. They're
long gone and as soon as we round up
my old man's stock, Jenkins and his
crew can be on their way. As for the
girl and Joe, we'll keep 'em close and
do the deal when Jenkins has gone."

"You reckon?"

Zach gritted his teeth at Tilly's mocking tone.

"That's what I reckon. Now get on and cook."

Zac was disturbed although he hid it from Tilly. She'd made him think. Tilly was shrewd and had an uncanny way of sizing up situations before. It always infuriated him to be outsmarted by a woman and it just might be that what she had said was true of Jenkins. For a start, the bastard had brought along more men than Zach had figured. He'd already found that he was treading warily and he didn't like it.

He stalked out of the cookhouse and went to find Jenkins. He heard sounds coming from the barn and went to see what was going on.

He found several of Jenkins's men crowding around while Pete himself was beating hell out of one of the prisoners. He saw it was his nephew, the one they called the white Indian. Although his fists were still bound with thongs he'd managed to get in a couple of double-fisted punches and Jenkins's left eye was swelling rapidly. As Zach entered the barn he was just in time to see Joe arch his back and draw up his legs and kick the air out of Jenkins's guts.

The boy could surely fight against all odds. Against his better judgement he felt a glow of family pride. But it only lasted a second. The boy was an encumbrance. But he was angry too. If anyone should dish out the punishment it should be he and no one else.

"What the hell's going on?" he barked.

Jenkins instinctively reacted to the tone as to an officer. It gave Joe the edge and he swiftly swung his legs and his right boot along with his spur, caught Jenkins right between the legs. Jenkins coughed and groaned and folded up.

Then Zach was reaching down and dragging Joe to his feet. He rocked on his heels nearly bringing them both down.

"Well? What happened?"

"I asked this piece of dogshit for help for Danny. He needs his wounds cleaning. He said it didn't matter. We were all gonners anyway. So I figured that if that was so, I might as well get stuck in." Joe laughed. "You can picture his face when he realized I was loose. If he'd been a bit longer in coming I'd have had my fists free. He made the mistake of not searching us for knives. Danny always carried a knife between his shoulder-blades. All Indians do. Very remiss of an ex-sergeant, don't you think?"

"Why are you telling me all this?"

"Because no man or beast is totally bad. I was brought up to respect even the most ferocious animal as having some spark of goodness in him."

"And?"

"I expect you to help Danny."

For a long moment Zach and Joe eyed each other. Zach, speculative, Joe, proud and challenging. At last Zach dropped his eyes. He nodded to one of the watching men.

"Fetch Tilly, she'll know what to do, and fasten this jasper good and tight and keep an eye on trim." As he walked out of the barn, Joe's laughter followed him.

For some reason that laughter bothered him. It was as if Joe knew something he didn't and it amused him. But what? There was no chance of a rescue. Parker's men were on the trail of their cows and would be gone at least three days and in that time anything could happen.

He was uneasy however and that made him short-tempered.

He found Perce and Rufus playing craps with Parker's crippled wrangler, an old man past his best but useful for yard chores. He was bald and toothless and most of the time he looked cross-eyed because of a crack on the head from a horse's hoof. But it didn't affect his skill at craps and the two men welcomed the interruption.

"You two fellers owe me two bucks and twenty cents," he quavered.

"You didn't really think we'd pay up, old-timer?" Rufus said, puffing up his big frame.

Old Nolly looked up at him and smiled uncertainly and backed down.

"I was only joking, fellers. No sweat!"

"Right! Then git!" Nolly scuttled away muttering to himself. Rufus grinned.

"Silly old fool! But he sure can shoot craps. Now, boss, what's a' doing? You look as if you've lost a buck and found a cent."

"It's Joe. I have a bad feeling about him."

"Then Perce and me will use him for target practice. Say the word and we'll tote him out of earshot and feed him to the buzzards."

"No! I want him alive for the time being. I want to send him back to my old man . . . Just watch him and don't go to sleep on the job or I'll have your guts!"

"OK . . . OK, boss. We'll watch him and the others. One move and all hell will be popping."

"Good. Now what about Parker, Perce? How's he doing?"

"He'll live. Looks worse than what he is. He'll not be able to move for a few days but he'll be OK."

Zach grunted. "As long as he can sign a money draft, I don't care about the rest. I'll talk to him tomorrow."

"You'll have to watch your back, boss," Rufus butted in. "It was a mistake leaving Jenkins alive. You should have finished him off when you had the chance."

"I can take him any time but his men are the problem. Believe me, Rufe, I've got the problem well in hand."

"I hope so, boss. I sure hope so!"

Zach frowned. "You two aren't thinking of two-timing me?"

Rufus managed to grin. "Now what gave you that idea, boss?"

"I know you, Rufe. I detect just a little doubt and when you doubt you forget where your loyalties lie."

"Now, boss, would I light out now just when you need me?"

"It all depends on Jenkins. Has he been talking to you?"

"Never a word, boss. I swear it."

"I hope that's true, Rufe. We've been friends on and off for a long time. I wouldn't like anything to get in the way of our friendship. You know what I mean, Rufe?"

"Yes, boss, I sure do but I might put it on record, that two-timing you had never crossed my mind . . . until now!"

Zach eyed him suspiciously and Rufus grinned and Zach nodded, not entirely convinced. Rufe might be playing a little game of his own.

It would pay him to get on with his plan, share the proceeds of Parker's cows with Jenkins, always considering Jenkins was on the level, and then light out with young Joe and the girl and hole up nice and tight and wait for Parker to pay up for his daughter and for his father to dig deep for his grandson and it would be then that he, Zach, would decide whether to send the boy back dead or alive.

He would give much to see his old man's face when he received his message. He would send it via the two cowpuncher prisoners . . .

He was pleased with his plan, but he wished he hadn't opened his big mouth to Tilly. He would have to go and sweet talk her so she would keep quiet. He'd rest easier if the business with Jenkins was complete and the bastard was out of his life.

He found both Tilly and Annie attending to Danny. Annie held him down while Tilly cleaned his wound which was showing red around the edges. It was surely infected by lead poisoning. He for one wouldn't be carrying no message back to his old man. It would have to be up to the Swede.

"Tilly, I want to talk to you. Let the girl finish the bandaging."

Tilly faced him furiously.

"Can't you see? The man is half crazy. It's taking Annie all her time to keep him quiet. If you would unloosen Joe's hands he could hold him. He's safe enough. You've got 'em all fastened to the wall by their necks. They're not going to run anywhere!"

Zach watched her broodingly as she wrapped white linen torn from the back of one of Parker's shirts around the wound. She didn't look very loving. Zach guessed she was seething with anger. It had been a mistake to slap her.

"I'm sorry, Tilly," he said abruptly as if the apology was torn from him.

"For what? For being the bastard you are? I would never have come out here if I'd known I was to be a goddamned slavey for a bloody murderer!"

"Be careful, Tilly. That's fighting talk!"

"I don't care a damn! In all the years

98

we've been together I never expected this! You said it would be easy. You were going home to your pa and to a better life. It was to be the end of racketing about. We were to settle down . . ."

"Yeh . . . yeah . . . yeah . . . I said all that and meant it."

"What about Jenkins? You were in cahoots with him even then!"

Zach sighed. "He was to be my last big deal. Jenkins wanted to get even with Parker and I wanted a stake. It seemed to be the logical thing to do 'specially when I found out about young Joe here. He turned all my plans round, Tilly. Surely you can see that?"

"I'll admit I was shocked. The situation has changed."

Joe looked from one to the other.

"Do you mind? You're talking as if I'm deaf and dumb!"

"Oh, shut up, you little interloper!"

Zach stalked off leaving the two women to finish strapping Danny up.

Danny opened his eyes and grinned.

"You sure do get under that feller's skin, Miss Tilly."

"You mean to say all that groaning and struggling was put on?"

"It sure was and it paid off. I'm sorry, Miss Annie, if I gave you a tough time."

Annie's eyes twinkled.

"I did wonder because holding you wasn't as bad as it looked." She looked at Tilly. "You won't tell that awful man, will you?"

"No, and what's more . . . " — she looked about her to see that no one was lurking nearby, then lowered her voice — "I'm leaving here tonight and you're all coming with me!"

All eyes were on her. Joe spoke for the rest.

"You mean you're going to free us?"

"Yes, but I'll do it after dark just in case he comes back again. I've already spoken to . . . " She paused. There was a rustle in the upper loft where the hay was stored. "What's that?"

"Probably a rat," Joe said easily. "We've seen a few about. They're after the horse feed."

Tilly still looked uneasy. She shivered.

"God knows what he would do if he finds out."

Annie squeezed her hand.

"I'll cover for you if something happens. I couldn't leave Pa. I'll have to stay."

"No!" Joe burst out. "You must come with us!" He looked at the pretty girl he remembered so well. "Annie, your father would want you to come. It would make it easier when we begin the assault on them. They could use you as a stand-off. You wouldn't want that?"

"Oh, Joe, I can't leave him! He's helpless. It's his spine as well as all the bruising. I must stay!" She started to cry.

Tilly put an arm about her.

"Hush now and don't get upset or Zach and Jenkins will wonder what's happening. You've got to act as you've never acted before and we'll talk about what you'll do later. Come on, we must go."

They left the barn and the shadowy figure crouched overhead stealthily and slowly came down the ladder and slipped away to find Pete Jenkins.

Joe's belly rumbled and he was stiff. He eased himself in the darkness. A chink of moonlight came through a knot in the rough plank door. He calculated it must be well after midnight.

He could hear Danny moving restlessly. The Swede slept, snoring heavily. Trust Big Hans to sleep at a time like this! But he had no nerves did Hans. He was all brawn and let nothing get in the way of his sleep.

Joe lay with every nerve on edge. He was waiting for that first sign that Tilly was coming. He didn't like the idea of a woman making the plans. Anything could go wrong and there would only be one chance.

Then it came. The scrape of a boot.

Something was wrong. Damnit! He should have insisted she cut them loose and let them take their chances. He sighed. Danny was the one to benefit by waiting and gathering his strength. The noise came again, closer this time. He screwed himself up to lash out.

"Night Stalker? Can you hear me?" the hoarse voice whispered. Joe felt his muscles relax. He recognized old Nolly, the cripple who long years ago had known his father, Grey Wolf, had saved Nolly's life when he and his horse had plunged into a swollen river. They had become friends over the years, and Joe and Nolly had recognized each other when Joe and the others had been brought to the ranch.

The knowledge that he had a friend out there had sustained Joe. He'd known Nolly would help them when the time was right.

"Nolly? Over here in the corner to the right of the door."

He heard the blundering steps and

the soft curses as Nolly felt his way across the barn. Joe kicked Hans who snorted and then came awake grabbing for a weapon that wasn't there.

"What the . . . what is it?" he gasped and then kicked out as Nolly fell over him. "Who the hell's that?"

"Be quiet, you bloody fool," Nolly croaked. "You've nearly done for me you big hulk! I've come to free you."

"What about Tilly?" Joe whispered.

"Jenkins got wind of something. Grabbed both her and the girl and fastened them up in the girl's bedroom."

"That must have been the rat we heard," Hans opined. "What we do now? Get in and get 'em out?"

"Let's get out first. Come on, Nolly, show a light and let's get at it."

Nolly struck a match fearful of being seen from outside and saw a battered lamp hanging from a hook. He lit it and shaded it with his fingers as it flared up. Then, taking a knife he quickly cut Joe's thongs about his wrists and neck and Joe took the knife and quickly freed the others as Nolly held the shaded lamp.

At once Joe was conscious of the pain in his hands as the circulation began to throb in his fingers. The others were similarly affected.

"Jees!" The big Swede gritted. "I feel as if I'll never grip a gun again!"

"You will. In the meanwhile, find a shovel or a rake and hit anything that moves. Danny, can you go find some horses and have 'em ready for us at the back of here?"

"Yes, boss. I'll do it or bust!"

Joe put a hand on his arm.

"You're what my father, Grey Wolf, would call a real dog of war!"

Danny grinned. "It takes more than a bullet to stop a Kiowa Apache!" They grinned at each other. They understood and respected each other.

Then Joe and Hans, followed by Nolly who lagged behind, quietly crept across the yard and to the back of the ranch-house. Nolly gestured to a window to the right. It was where Tilly and Annie were being held. Joe nodded and picked up a stave of wood. He hefted it. It was well balanced as a weapon.

He was examining the window frame when a dog barked and they both dropped to a crouch. Joe cursed under his breath. Then a boot scraped the veranda and a figure appeared smoking a cigarette. The dog had saved them from walking into trouble.

"Be quiet, damn you!" a harsh voice called and Joe recognized it for Pete Jenkins. So the bastard was waiting. A yelp came from the dog which turned to a soft whine. "Fasten the bloody thing up, Jake, and take a turn around the buildings and look in on the prisoners and see that they're all nice and snug."

"Yes, boss." Jake called the dog and cursed as he tried to catch him. Both dog and man ran furiously around the corner.

Joe waited for the right moment and the wooden stave crashed down on the unsuspecting man's head. Joe caught him as he fell and dragged him into the shadows. The dog ran into the night.

Quickly reaching for the man's gun, Joe moved on. He waved to Hans.

"Watch out for reinforcements. See if you can get a gun. I'm going round the other side." With that he crouched low and keeping to the shadows came up behind a second man on the other side of the ranch-house who was drinking out of a bottle.

He never knew when the bottle fell from his nerveless fingers. Joe acquired a second Colt. Now he was ready.

A muffled cry alerted him to the fact that Hans hadn't had it too easy. Then a shot came and Zach and Pete Jenkins charged out of the door, guns blazing as all hell let loose. Joe joined in with a couple of shots and then went in to seek out the women.

The door was barred but not locked. It didn't take a minute to undo and inside he found Tilly and a frightened

Annie who stood in front of a cot where her father lay.

"Come on, you've got to get out! We've not much time."

Tilly grabbed a rifle with a businesslike hand.

"I'm ready. Come on, kid. You can't help your father. He's a goner . . . you'll have to come with us."

"No! I can't leave him!"

Parker's hand came up feebly and waved to the door.

"Take her . . . I'm finished . . . my spine . . . " He coughed and Joe could see he was having trouble breathing.

"I'll look after her, sir." With that he caught Annie roughly and gave her a smart tap on the jaw and then slung her over his shoulders. Tilly looked at him admiringly.

"I wouldn't like to argue with you!"

"Quit talking and move!"

Outside they could hear shots and shouts as Hans and Nolly kept up a barrage in the shadows. They could hear Jenkins cursing as Hans moved from point to point after each blast. He was clearly enjoying himself.

Joe hauled Tilly by the hand and dragged her behind the barn as he carried Annie. There, four horses were milling about and Danny leaning up against the barn wall, his chest heaving.

"Come on, wardog! Don't give up now!" Danny grinned and staggered to his horse and held it while Joe flung a dazed Annie aboard.

"Danny, help Tilly up, will you? I'm going to look for Hans." He didn't wait for an answer.

But it was too late. He was just in time to see Hans throw up his weapon and crash to the ground. Then with a howl which was like the baying of hounds. Zach and Pete Jenkins turned on Joe. He snapped off a shot which missed and then dodged the answering hail of bullets. He turned and ran and was aboard his own horse before Zach and Jenkins could reach the corner.

Then giving an Apache yell, he sent the horse off at a gallop and they swept into the yard and out of it before the rest of the cowboys knew what was happening.

But it was Zach who calmly drew a bead on the galloping horses and it was Tilly he was aiming for. She gave a piercing cry and Joe saw the red bloodstain cover her back. She was dead before she hit the ground.

Annie's horse faltered, but Joe swore and lashed out at it and it lengthened its stride. Danny cursed but hung on while Tilly's horse racing free bumped against its stable mate, crushing his leg.

Behind them came the thunder of hooves and Joe spurred the horses to greater effort. Gradually Danny slowed down. Great gouts of blood were now shooting from his wound.

"You go on," he shouted. "I'll hold them off as long as possible." He didn't wait for an answer but guided his animal up a small spur of rock. He fell off and staggering to his feet gave the beast a mighty swipe on the rump. It galloped away and he settled himself behind a rock to wait for the oncoming men.

He knew he couldn't stop them for long. But if he could get the bastard Pete Jenkins or the young boss's uncle he would be satisfied . . .

They came sooner than he expected. He snapped off every slug in the gun. His sight was blurring. It was getting dark but he knew that he was taking someone with him. He heard the yell and sensed rather than saw a man fall. He smiled. It was a good way for a wardog to die . . .

6

THEY had been travelling for hours. Annie's head hung low, the pain in her jaw now just a dull ache. She was aware of following Joe, her eyes dully focused on the broad rear of his horse. They were travelling upwards but she was too tired to care where they were going. Every muscle in her body ached which took her mind from her jaw.

The moon was well up when finally the horse in front stopped. She was aware of gentle hands lifting her down. Her legs felt like jelly.

"Where are we?"

"In the foothills of the Santa Ynez mountains."

"We seem to have been travelling forever."

"Don't worry. We're travelling in a circle. I'm taking you to my

112

grandfather's spread where you will be safe."

"How long will that take?"

"Three . . . four days if all goes well. Now sit down and rest while I light a fire."

"How will you do that?" He smiled.

"The Indian way, with two dry sticks."

"Oh!" She watched him curiously as he crouched down to make a pile of dry grass and twigs into a bonfire shape. "I never thought I'd ever see you again," she murmured softly. "I missed you when you went away."

"I missed you too. You were the only white person who cared enough to help me. I was a confused kid in those days. You helped me to come to terms with what I am."

"And now?"

"I'm a white Indian. Didn't you know? That is how people see me."

"I don't see you like that."

"No, because you're different."

"I see you as a person in your own right."

"Thank you." He answered abruptly and she wondered what was wrong. "Are you cold?" he said as the little bonfire burst into flame. "It gets cold up here in these hills during the night." She shivered a little. Then he stripped off his jacket and put it about her shoulders. "I'll have to leave you and forage around for more wood."

"But you too will be cold! I couldn't possibly . . . "

He put a rough hand over her mouth.

"I'm used to wearing no clothes, remember? Now keep warm. I'll be back before the fire dies down."

He kept his word. The fire was low and the ashes turning from red to pink and grey when he returned with an armful of wood and a jack-rabbit. He grinned when he came to stand over her.

"See . . . I haven't lost the old skills. We'll have a fine supper and there's a small stream just beyond the ridge where you can wash. What more do we want?"

Later, after the horses had been watered and hobbled for the night and the fire coaxed into a blazing mass and the half-charred rabbit eaten, Annie's head slipped on to Joe's shoulder and she slept.

It was the agitated twittering of birds that awakened Joe from a light doze. He'd stayed awake most of the night but as dawn approached he'd allowed himself to relax.

Now he was awake and fully alert. Annie stirred at his sudden movement.

"What is it?" she asked sleepily.

"I'm not sure. I think someone's coming. I'm going to take a look-see."

"Why? How do you know?"

He looked upwards. "The birds," he answered succinctly and moved away with the careful light tread of an Indian.

He climbed a boulder and at the top crouched and looked back from the way they had come. The sun's rays blinded him but soon he could see a cloud of dust which could only mean horsemen. He wasted no time but slithered down the rough stone and back to Annie.

"We'll have to go. They're following our trail." He kicked the burnt wood ash into the ground. "Quick! Cover the ash with dead leaves while I saddle the horses!"

He was soon back leading the horses. He had stripped off his shirt and she saw with surprise that one horse now wore a set of pads covering its hooves.

"Take off your petticoat," he demanded brusquely. She hesitated.

"Come, this is no time to be modest. I must pad the other horse's hooves." He gathered up dried grass as she turned her back and shrugged herself out of her petticoat. She handed it to him wordlessly and watched as he tore it into four pieces and he was binding each hoof, surely and swiftly.

Then he swung her up into her saddle.

"Ready?" She nodded although her

116

legs ached and her bottom felt the bruising of last night's trek. "Then we're ready to ride as you've never ridden before." Bending down he reached for the rope fastened to her mount, he kicked his own horse in the ribs and leapt forward. Annie gasped as she felt the powerful spring of the horse between her legs.

Then followed a hellish nightmare ride which Annie would never forget for the rest of her life. It seemed to go on forever. The trail was forever upwards and twice they left it to take advantage of short cuts and yet when Joe stopped to ease the horses and climb up on to a ridge, the bunch of men was still trailing behind.

Joe cursed. It was evident that Pete Jenkins had one of the Indian ex-army scouts with him. Whoever he was, he was skilled at his job. Relentlessly they came on. He saw Annie was exhausted. It would only be a matter of time before they overtook them unless he could come up with some plan.

His mind worked swiftly. They were now coming into familiar country where he'd lived as a boy. If he could make the Colorado River there were places where no white man had ever been. He could hide her and lure those sons of bitches away.

He decided it was worth a try.

"Can you ride a little longer?"

She gritted her teeth. There was no way she would admit to her weakness.

"Yes, as long as necessary." But he noted her slight hesitation. He drew up so suddenly his mount backed on his haunches and the other animal cannoned into him before stopping. Joe was off his horse in a flash and up behind Annie before she knew what was happening.

"What . . . what are you doing?" she stammered.

"Giving my horse a rest. You can lean back now, Annie, and relax and you can shut your eyes and rest yourself."

"But I could manage . . . "

"The horses need to rest. Soon, we'll change mounts and give this beast a rest. It's an old Apache trick. They can ride long distances without stopping by changing mounts. Now relax because we're leaving the trail for good. We're heading for the Colorado River."

The horses moved at a gentle but sustaining trot which they could keep up for hours. The rhythm was soothing and, incredibly, Annie slept. It was hunger and a change of rhythm that finally awakened her. They were carefully picking their way down a steep slope.

"Where are we?" she murmured, still confused with sleep.

"Coming down to the river." He sounded quite cheerful. She twisted in his arms to look up at him.

"But what about getting across?"

"No need for that. I know a place for you to hide and rest. An Indian refuge. You'll be safe."

"And you?"

"I'm going after a snake. Cut off its

head and the rest will die!"

"But I'll be alone!"

"No, you'll have company. I'm taking you to an old shaman who lives alone in these hills. The place is called Whitewater Falls and he is a very kind wise old man. He will make you welcome."

And it was so. Joe, leading the two horses with Annie drooping on her mount's back, finally arrived at a small creek running into the great fast-flowing river. They travelled up it for a short while and then Annie saw the Whitewater Falls, a roaring mass of water which flung its spray high into the air. It was a narrow silver gash of water with high cliffs on both sides. It tumbled for more than a hundred feet into the stream below. Annie gasped at its beauty and gazed at it with awe.

Then, as if he'd known he was to have visitors, an old man appeared from somewhere behind the curtain of water. He stood on a black rock perpetually wet from the spray. He held up an arm in greeting. Joe responded and waited. The old man disappeared.

Soon he reappeared down below and slowly and painfully with the aid of a stout stick, came to stand before them.

"What brings you here, Night Stalker, and with a women?" His glance encompassed them both.

"I seek your help, Seeker-after-Truth. I would ask that you care for this girl until my return."

"And why should you leave her?"

"Because she is in danger from white marauders who would hold her to ransom."

"And what is your interest in this?"

"The man who leads the marauders is my enemy. He is the one who killed Grey Wolf and Blue Cloud. Need I say more?"

The old man looked grave and he nodded.

"You have an obligation to them. They will sleep better if you deal with this man. The time is right. Come, you

121

can hobble the horses behind that rock over there and then I shall show you my dwelling place."

Joe quickly removed saddles and examined the horses' feet. He watered them and left them munching contentedly on the lush green grass surrounding them.

Then he and Annie followed the old man up a narrow trail scarcely noticeable except for expert eyes. It wound up and behind rock with the waterfall plunging and eternally racing down one side and stunted trees clinging to the rock on the other. It was an amazing climb and as they ascended higher, Annie turned pale and clung on to Joe.

He couldn't speak to her, the roar of the fall blotted out all communication. He put an arm about her and patted her shoulder and reassured she moved slowly ahead.

Then suddenly the old man in front wasn't there any more. Joe hesitated and then moved Annie along and then the reason for the shaman's disappearance was revealed. He'd stepped into a crevice behind a jutting rock and there it was, the perfect home for a recluse, a dry cave which was actually a split in the rock formation.

Joe drew Annie inside. The silence with only a muted roar from the fall made their ears ache. Seeker-after-Truth was already lighting a home-made candle made from animal fat. He was an impressive figure in his own dwelling. He seemed to swell in stature. The yellow glow cast shadows on the wrinkled bronze face likening it to a carving in teak. The long grey hair was parted above his brow and plaited and secured with strips of deerskin. He wore an amulet about his neck and circlets of feathers hung from a belt at his waist. His moccasins and trousers were of deerskin and he wore a jerkin made of buffalo hide with the fur on the inside. His arms were bare and muscular for such an old man. Joe was impelled to bow to him. He responded with dignity.

"Welcome to my home. What I have is yours. Please, make yourself comfortable." He motioned to Annie to sit on a pile of ancient buffalo skins that smelled strangely to her nostrils.

Gratefully she sat down. She wanted to cry with exhaustion but controlled herself. She bit her lip until it hurt. She couldn't . . . wouldn't let Joe see her weep like some namby-pamby city girl. Joe's regard was important to her.

She listened to the murmur of voices and gradually she slept.

Seeker-after-Truth looked at Joe gravely.

"You are determined to do this thing?"

"I am. It is just as important to me to avenge my natural parents' death as it is to avenge Grey Wolf and Blue Cloud."

Seeker-after-Truth nodded.

"I am glad you think that way. It shows you are well balanced. That you are truly midway between one culture and another. You, my friend, have a mission in life. You will go back after your revenge is completed and all the poison it generated is erased from your spiritual self. You will fight all your life to bring the Indian and the white man closer together. I see it all in the flames from the fire."

With those words he threw a substance on to the small fire in the cave. At once blue flames leapt high in the air.

"See for yourself, your future, Night Stalker. You cannot escape it." Joe stared into the flames and swirling shapes danced before him. He saw a sea of faces all looking at him as he spoke with passion. He saw angry faces and smiling faces and fists waving and hands clapping and a myriad other shapes and colours and behind it all he saw Annie . . .

He blinked and when he looked at the old man he was smiling.

"Yes, I see you had a glimpse of your future and as for the woman I shall look after her well. But now you must go through the purifying rituals. You must not seek revenge with a heart full of past hates. You must strip away your old self like a snake sloughs off its skin. That way you will have the spirits with you and your revenge will turn into judgement and a fit punishment."

Joe bowed to him again.

"I leave myself in your hands."

"Then come with me to my most holy place." Joe followed him out of the cave and they climbed higher up the trail until they came to a platform of rock left long ago by a giant landslide. There was a breathtaking view of the surrounding hills and a man could watch the sun rise in the east or see it set in the west.

There was a hearthstone set in the middle and around it carved symbols had been etched into the soft stone. Joe saw the sun, moon and stars in all their phases and now Seeker-after-Truth made him stand before the symbol of the full sun.

"You must strip naked while I

prepare the incense and then you will repeat the invocation after me."

Joe watched as the shaman took certain herbs from his amulet pouch and placed them in a certain way on the hearthstone, and all the while he muttered to himself. Joe had heard Grey Wolf talk of the rituals the old man had used in times gone by but had never experienced them himself. He knew how Grey Wolf had revered Seeker-after-Truth and spoken of him with awe. He knew he was a privileged being. He only hoped he could live up to the old man's trust in him.

He was ready when the shaman looked at him. He smiled.

"I see you have said your Christian prayer."

Joe started. "Yes, I suppose it was a prayer of sorts. How did you know?"

"I know. A prayer is not something that is just said. It travels, it leaves the supplicant and sends out ripples like a pebble thrown in a still pond. For one who knows, a prayer is easy to intercept.

Now come, we shall commence. You shall face the east and raise your arms for you are preparing yourself for a rebirth. Your past and its negativity will be carried away in the incense which will enfold you. You will repeat after me . . . "

The small bunch of carefully placed herbs suddenly burst into flame with a light crackling and sizzling. At once Joe breathed in the pungent scent and in his imagination it was all around and in him. He was part of it. He *was* it!

As at a great distance he heard the shaman's words clearly and slowly and he repeated them, mystical words of which he had no knowledge but they felt and sounded right. He was comfortable with them. He trusted Seeker-after-Truth.

Then the voice receded as if he, Joe, was being whisked away into other realms of existence. He was conscious of vague grey shapes whispering in his ear, truths he couldn't quite grasp but knew he would remember when the time was right. Then he was whirling away, a speck of energy in an endless universe and suddenly he was back standing with his arms raised high and the blue-grey smoke of the incense dispersing leaving behind the sickly sweet-sour smell of burnt herbs. He opened his eyes. Seeker-after-Truth was watching him intently.

"So you have come back from your journey. You have all the answers you will ever need. Come, the ritual is nearly over. You must stand in the waterfall and wash away the last of your negativity and you will be as a new-born spirit."

Joe followed the old man to the very top of the waterfall where it fell over the ledge and down into the chasm below. His heart beat fast as he contemplated the flow and strength of the water. Seeker-after-Truth smiled.

"Take heart. Your fear is your last negativity and your imagination makes it appear harder than it is. Have no fear, my son, you will find it quite an experience."

Joe took a deep breath and took a step into the water. His foot sought and found a smooth slippery surface and taking courage he stepped out. The water flowed and gurgled about his ankles. Then with surprise he found that there were a series of steps and he moved downwards until he was awash with water and he sat down as if on a stool and the water cascaded over him.

He was conscious of a great relaxing of his body. It was exhilaratingly cold and his blood leapt and every part of him felt as if renewed. It was an ecstasy that hurt.

Then, as if a voice whispered in his ear, he knew it was time to move. He felt a reluctance. He knew he would never again reach the heights he'd reached today.

He clambered out of the water, his body pulsing and his mind ready for whatever he might face. He smiled at

Seeker-after-Truth.

"Now I am truly ready."

Down below in the cave, Seeker-after-Truth prepared food. There was yesterday's stew and cornbread. Joe ate and when Annie awakened, she joined him. She sensed there was something different about him but couldn't put a name to it.

Then the time came for him to depart. He held her close.

"Don't be afraid. I'll come back for you and remember, Seeker-after-Truth is your friend."

She nodded and on impulse put her arm about his neck and kissed him.

"I'll be waiting for you," and she blushed.

Joe thought of her all the way down the trail and when he finally saddled the horses, he looked upwards but did not see any sign of her. But she was watching him from the holy place and her prayer went with him.

7

FOR two days Joe had hardly been out of the saddle. The skin bag of pemmican which Seeker-of-Truth had provided was nearly done. He was weary as were the two horses he rode alternately. Now he paused to water the animals at a small stream and he chewed on a strip of dried meat as they drank their fill.

He heard the faint unmistakable sound of gunfire coming in on the breeze from the south. At once both horses lifted their heads and their ears twitched as they blew through their nostrils. Joe tightened the girths and prepared to ride. Maybe he was in luck and the sound might lead him to the men he sought.

The trail led him over dry stony ground sparsely covered in scrub. He knew he was riding in the right direction. Jenkins would by now be heading for the railroad track. It was a matter of crossing his tracks and even a blind man could read the spoor of a thousand head of cattle.

He stopped at the head of a narrow valley. Puffs of smoke came from a small cabin set well back beside a small stand of cottonwoods. Answering fire came from the trees and the scrub. There were no sign of cows being pastured, so this little mess was nothing to do with Jenkins, Joe considered.

But whoever was in the cabin was hard pressed for only one gun appeared to be spitting bullets while at least three gunmen were out there exchanging shots.

It was time to take a hand.

He dismounted and walked his horses to the nearest cover and then proceeded on foot. He fingered his knife for he was short on bullets and would need them later. But he was as much at home with a knife as he was with any weapon. He moved forward stealthily, his muscles well balanced and his feet coming down with care so as not to dislodge even the smallest pebble. Then, watching from where the puffs of smoke came from he moved in a circle and came up behind the nearest assailant.

Joe recognized him as a typical comanchero, a guerilla left over from the wars, a parasite who roamed the country, robbing and stealing to survive, a wild animal of a man. He reckoned the others would be no better.

"Hi, there! Looking for trouble?" He crouched low on the rock above the man and when he turned with a start, Joe's knife thudded into his chest. The man's eyes widened and blood poured from his mouth and he collapsed like a rag doll.

Joe stood over him but felt no compunction. He'd died as he'd lived, giving and receiving no quarter.

He quickly relieved the body of weapons and ammo. Whoever he was prided himself on his selection of weapons having an Army Spencer repeater rifle and a couple of business-like Colt .45s. Joe grinned and shrugged on the twin bandoleers and felt like a walking army.

Then, recovering his knife and wiping it clean on the man's shirt he moved on. He hoped it would be as easy with the next one. But this time the man dressed in ragged army uniform heard his approach and with a snarl turned and snapped off a shot which buzzed past Joe's ear like an angry hornet and made Joe leap for cover.

Then shots were traded and Joe cursed. It wouldn't be long before reinforcements came along. Whoever was out there would become curious. So Joe resorted to an old Indian trick. He snapped off two shots and rolled and then came up on his elbows and bellied forward towards his enemy while hugging the undergrowth and following the lay of the land.

Then rising up not ten yards from

the man who was still blazing away at the spot where he'd been, Joe raised his knife and it hurtled end over end, silent and deadly and thudded into the outlaw's back. He went down without a cry.

Joe hefted the broad Bowie knife clear and was in the act of cleaning it when the third man sprang at him from behind. It was the faintest hint of buffalo fat that saved him and the inner sense that someone was watching him that made him turn and meet the half-breed head on. His facial features and body ornaments proclaimed him of Cheyenne blood.

Lips curled back and a long knife scything the air, the man leapt at him, arm swinging and a blood-curdling cry issuing from his lips. The knife was already bloodied. Joe dived beneath him landing on his back as he twisted to slice the assailant's legs.

He drew blood and the man howled with fury and then Joe was fighting for his life, two blades clashing together as they attacked and counterattacked. Joe was conscious of a gash in his left forearm and hot blood trickling down to his hand. He felt a wave of fury washing over him and his adrenalin doubled. Snarling as a maddened wolf would do when cornered, he flexed his muscles and caught the half-breed around the throat and squeezed. The man threshed beneath him and twice Joe lost control and the deadly knife swung at him. But each time he evaded the thrust and he sensed that the man was weakening.

Then as suddenly as it had begun it was finished. The half-breed gave a great cry and he heaved himself upright dragging Joe with him and it was as if his life force left him on that long last breath. He collapsed and Joe's fingers locked about his throat and stayed locked until he was convinced the man was dead. Then he rolled away from him and lay still, chest heaving and sweat pouring from him and mingling with his blood.

He lay a long time and then realized he must bind up his wound before he bled to death. He stumbled upright and made his way towards the cabin. A rifle butt poked from a window.

"Stay right there, mister. Who are you?"

Joe stood still and slowly raised his hands rocking back on his heels.

"I'm Joe Adams."

"You're the one who stopped those bastards?"

"Yeh, you might say that."

"Are they dead?"

"They were when I saw 'em last. A comanchero and an ex-army feller and a half-breed. Any more about?"

"Nope! And you can come right in, mister. You look as if you need bandaging."

A man of fifty-odd years, lean and mean with a balding grey head stepped outside, his rifle at the ready, just in case.

Joe took several steps and then cursed and fell to his knees. The man dropped his rifle and ran forward, shouting as he did so.

"Hey, Hank, get out here! We've got a wounded man on our hands!" A boy of about twelve came running towards them while a small girl of about eight years stood shyly in the doorway, her tear stained face betraying the ordeal they had been through.

"I'm Eddie Fenshawe and this is Hank and that's my daughter, Alice. I'm sure owing you thanks, mister. I thought we was all finished, until I realized something was happening out there. I prayed to God, and by all that's holy, you came along. Come on now, let's get that arm bandaged."

"The half-breed . . . his knife was bloodied . . . "

"Yeh, that bastard killed my dog before we knew they were there. Heard the dog bark and then yelp. It wasn't like Wolf to yelp and so I got the kids inside and I forted up, but I couldn't have lasted that long. I was running out of ammunition."

Joe watched while the arm was bandaged. It was sore and would be stiff tomorrow, but he'd live.

"Those jaspers have plenty of weapons and ammo. I've taken what was on the comanchero but you can have the rest. Have you seen a cattle drive in the last few days? I'm looking for an outfit."

Eddie Fenshawe was hustling up some grub. He paused.

"Yeh, two days ago, driving southwest. Why you looking for them, mister?"

"They're rustlers and I'm after them for other reasons."

"Oh! I thought it funny that they should risk the dead man's lands. Not much water out that way for a big herd. There was plenty dust as they moseyed along."

"So they're not pushing them?"

"Naw. They looked as if they had all the time in the world. Nursing 'em, they were."

"Thanks for the tip."

"You're welcome. Now come and

eat. It's rough but I do the best I can."

"Got no wife?"

"No. Emma caught a fever and died six months ago. There's only me and the kids. We manage." His tone was brusque, dismissive.

Joe looked at the watching youngsters, silent, curious, occasionally scratching their tousled hair, their thin white faces betraying the conditions they were living under.

"Any close neighbours?"

"Nope! Closest is old Pete Marley who scratches a living ten miles away. Funny old geyser. He don't like company so we don't see him much."

"What about your children? Have they been to school?"

"Nope! Their ma taught 'em their letters and they read bits out of the Bible, and they can count enough to get by. We manage all right, mister."

"But not if you get other riders coming in with weapons at the ready.

You were lucky I was passing by."

"And I thank you right and proper for that, mister, but I be hoping lightning doesn't strike twice!"

"If I was those kids' pa, I'd be lighting out for town and to hell with it! I'd not gamble on my luck!"

"But this is our home! I've sweated buckets for this land and the chance to breed good cows. I've nigh on seventy head and all good stock. Someday I'll make it big. I feel it in my bones!"

"Well, I wish you luck, mister. But now I'll be on my way. I want to catch up with that herd."

"I'll give you some grub. It's the least I can do. There's some sour belly and bread and coffee if you want it. I just got in my supplies so I can give you sugar too."

"That's mighty kind of you. I'd appreciate coffee and sugar. But I've got no pot."

"Hell! I can soon give you a pot. The missis was a great one for collecting kitchen stuff. You sure have been travelling rough!"

They stood and waved as he rode off. He returned the gesture and without looking back made his way due south. Now he had a better idea where he would find the men he sought.

He wondered about Zach. Would he be with them or had he gone back to hassle old George? Then he put Zach out of his mind. He must find the herd and work around it and follow closely and see how many men and who they were who nursed them along.

The second morning he smelled them. The breeze was coming from the south and the scent was unmistakable. Somewhere ahead were cows herded together who cropped the grass as they went and were just as busy at the other end dropping it where it fell.

There was trail-dust too, wafting over the land turning everything a hazy grey. Joe found the heavy wagon tracks made by the chuckwagon and followed cautiously.

He figured he would hobble the

horses at night and do a little scouting when the men who weren't night-hawking were fed and at ease about their camp-fire. He could figure out just how strong the enemy was.

Gradually the distance lessened and he had the chuckwagon in view. A young boy was driving and an old balding man with stooped shoulders sat by him and regularly used his stetson to beat off the flies, his red checked shirt grey with dust. Not much danger from those two.

He rode well to the side of the wagon for somewhere just in front someone would be riding point with the lead animals moving ahead.

He was right. Over the next ridge he came on them, a long slow, winding snake of animals who bellowed, threw up their heads and did what cows do when close herded. He could see four men riding up and down the line at different points, bringing back stray mavericks into line and uniting calves with their mothers. So the bastards hadn't stopped to pick out steers ready for market, they'd taken all Parker's best breeding stock.

Joe pondered as he watched the manoeuvres. So this lot weren't for the city's abattoirs. They were for some rancher who would pay good money for breeding stock. Or maybe Pete Jenkins figured to raise them himself on his own ranch. It was an interesting idea.

That night he ate a cold supper and watched and waited. The cows were bedded down and apart from the occasional lowing of the animals, all was quiet except the monotonous hum of the punchers on night patrol.

He knew the first watch would finish around midnight when others would take their place until dawn. It was a night to move around and check on who was there and where.

The fireglow was his target. He stripped, discarded everything but his trousers and his knife. This was a reconnoitre, not an onslaught. It was going to take patience if he was to take out Jenkins and the others. He smiled. He had patience. Grey Wolf had taught him that and taught him well.

He stepped carefully, watching for movement in the flickering shadows cast by the fire. The chuckwagon was close by and the old man was strumming a guitar and singing about lonely cowboys and the women they'd left behind.

Half a dozen men lounged close by, drinking beer or playing cards. Joe could see no look-out. They were confident and careless.

Suddenly Pete Jenkins appeared in the firelight buttoning up his jeans. Joe felt a rush of pure hatred at the sight of him. He balled his fists in an effort to control his emotions. It was then it became clear the difference between a white man and an Apache. Grey Wolf would have remained resolute but dispassionate. He, on the other hand, was reacting as would his white forebears.

He crouched low, watching, waiting. Forcing back emotion he made his move. Slowly, with each foot set down as delicately and deliberately as if walking on glass, he gradually neared the campfire until he could hear the low-toned conversation.

"How long now, boss, before we meet up with Slade?"

"A couple or three days. His outfit are going to be at Black Rock or thereabouts. They'll take over the herd and we can hightail it south." Then Joe heard the unforgettable laughter of Jenkins. It brought back memories of his capture when he, as a wild untamed Indian boy, faced the merciless sergeant who delighted not only in torturing prisoners but humiliating and bullying the soldiers in his platoon.

But it wasn't for his own suffering he was out seeking revenge but for the death of Grey Wolf and the sufferings of Blue Cloud before her death. Indians were just animals in Pete Jenkins's book.

Joe felt the old hate and tasted it on his tongue like acid.

He drew his knife. He was sorely tempted to end it here and now. But then he saw the unmistakable hunched figure of the cripple, the man called Perce, who rose awkwardly from the group playing cards.

"That's it, you, bastard! You've played us all for suckers, Zinnerman, so just bring out that ace up your sleeves or I'll plug you where you sit!" With a quick lithe movement, a gun glinted in his hand.

The little group froze. Then Pete Jenkins moved forward.

"Easy man! Do you realize what you're saying? Zinnerman is one of my best men. He's no cardsharp. Just because you lost your dough doesn't mean he's cheating!"

"Look him over yourself then," snarled Perce. "I know what I saw, damnit!"

Jenkins looked at Zinnerman.

"Is this true, Zinnerman? Are you on

148

the make? For if you are, it's the last hand you play!"

"Gee, boss, this feller isn't one of us . . . I reckoned it weren't no big deal."

"You mean he's right? You were cheating? How much?" Now the other two punchers were looking angry.

"I reckon a hundred altogether. I was going to pay Tosh and Cal back . . . "

"Like hell you were! You know my rules, Zinnerman. We trust each other!"

"It won't happen again, boss."

"Too right, it won't!" And before any of the onlookers guessed his intent, Jenkins drew his gun and Zinnerman slumped backwards, his bulging eyes showing the sudden fear as he faced the gun.

Joe drew in his breath sharply and waited.

Jenkins gave Perce an ingratiating smile.

"See, you're one of us now with Rufus. I said I would play fair and square with you if you joined us, and I'm a man who keeps his word. Now you keep your word. Tell me what Zach Adams had in mind."

Joe tensed. Zach must have copped it when Danny gave him and Annie a chance to get away. He heard Perce's chuckle.

"He was going to ransom old Adam's grandson when he caught him, and then when he got the dough, send the boy back tied to his horse. He thought it would be a good joke against his old man."

"Some feller," grunted Jenkins. "How do you suppose we catch this white Indian bastard? He's wily and he's tough. I know. I had him through my hands when he was a kid, but Parker took him and when he was rehabilitated, he was sent to his folks. I said at the time it was a mistake. White kids brought up by Indians stay Indian. It's a known fact."

"The old man thinks a lot of him. He's made him his heir so Zach said.

That was the trouble. Zach reckoned his pa would fall all over him to have him back. Instead, he was kicked out on his arse. He didn't like that, he wanted his pa to suffer."

"And when we find this feller he will," smiled Jenkins. "You're with me on this?"

"Yeh. Me and Rufe work together and we've no other plans. You play fair with us and we play fair with you. You need extra men seeing you've had your losses."

"You'll not share in the sale of these cows. You start picking up your share after this job's over. Right?"

"Fair enough. I reckon me and Rufe have got us a good deal and you can give us a bonus for putting you on to the Adams kid."

"OK. You drive a hard bargain but give Tosh and Cal their dough and all's square. We don't want trouble in the camp."

Joe watched as the men shared out the small piles of cash between them.

Perce hobbled away clearly still angry. Jenkins watched them go.

"If I were you, fellers, I'd steer clear of that jasper. He's dangerous in a sly kind of way. I don't like him but we need him and his pard . . . at least for now."

Cal drank from his bottle.

"I'm sorry about Zinnerman. He never done that to us before."

"Maybe he had his reasons. Maybe that punk pushed him too far. We'll never know but I had to take a stand, especially as he admitted it. You know the rules."

Cal nodded morosely. Tosh held his head down saying nothing.

"I suppose it's us who have to do the burying?"

"Yeh. Plant him right, boys. He deserves that."

Joe watched from the shadows as the digging began. Later, he saw the nighthawks come in. Rufe was with them. Seven fighting men altogether, nine if you counted the cook and the boy. He could take them all but he wasn't interested in the others. He wanted Jenkins and the little cripple and the man called Rufus. Then his real parents and Grey Wolf and Blue Cloud could rest in peace.

He watched Cal and Tosh ride out with Perce, humming softly as they ranged at a distance around the resting cows. A lifting head and a lonely bawl was all that could he heard in answer to the soft hum of the punchers.

Joe moved in closer. He took his time for time meant nothing to him. Rufus and Jenkins were somewhere close. If he was lucky he would get them both . . .

Rufus and the other two men settled by the fire after they'd eaten. There was little conversation. Neither Rufus or Perce were accepted by Jenkins's crew. They were still suspicious of them. They would have to earn the men's respect.

The moon was clouding over and the camp was quiet when Joe decided the time was right. Rufus's giant form was covered with a horseblanket and he began to snore. One of the men near him turned restlessly and settled again. Joe moved closer like a wraith hardly causing a stirring of leaves.

His arm was raised, knife gleaming as it flashed down, its target Rufus's back, when the first peal of thunder crashed all around them and the figures around the camp-fire awakened and grabbed for their guns.

Rufus opened his eyes in shock at the sound and twisted away from Joe as Joe's arm came down. He missed Rufus and the impetus of the move sent him sprawling. Rufus reacted and was on him before he could blink. It was then Joe realized Rufus had survived many bar-room brawls.

He fought mean and dirty. He was also fighting for his life.

But Joe too was fighting for his life. He was also fighting to avenge his parents and it gave him added strength.

They rolled and clawed each other in silent ferocity. It seemed an age but in reality it was only seconds because before the other men collected their wits and could see what was happening, it was all over. Joe's knife sliced through Rufus's throat like a knife through butter. If left a gaping wound like a huge blood red mouth. Joe's hand and chest were drenched in hot sticky blood.

He was aware of a singing in his heart. One down, two to go.

He was gone before the rest of the men crowded round the body.

Jenkins who had bedded down under the chuckwagon joined the men.

"What's all the fuss boys? It's just a thunder clap." Then he stared down at the body. "Jesus! What the hell's happened?"

"We don't rightly know, boss. There was this thunderclap and all hell broke loose. It was some Indian feller, nearly naked he was and him and Rufe was snarling over each other like two tom cats. Then he was gone. He was like a bleeding ghost, all silent-like."

Jenkins looked about him, white-faced and shaken.

"He could still be around."

"I doubt it, boss. But we can take a look-see."

"Yeh, you do that but take care."

"Could be some private feud we know nothing about. He'll be long gone by now."

"Hmm . . . I wonder." Jenkins walked thoughtfully away. Suddenly he was a very worried man. There was no more chance to sleep. He buckled on his gunbelt and sat with his back against the chuckwagon until the men returned to report no signs of a man within a two-mile radius.

It was a silent and chastened crew who moved the cattle on. The men were jumpy and Jenkins increasingly irritable. There were small signs that all was not as it should be. The cook lost a ladle and found it in the water butt. One of the men complained of losing his tobacco pouch and blamed his partner until it appeared in a mess of stew. Then one night the horses got free and had to be rounded up and a saddle went missing only to be found hanging from a tree branch.

They were spooked and they didn't like it. They blamed Perce as he'd been Rufus's partner. Jenkins kept quiet. He had his own suspicions and let the men believe it was Perce the unseen enemy was after.

Then Perce awoke one morning with a rattler staring him in the face. He screamed and as the snake drew back to strike, he rolled aside and, sweating, scrabbled for his gun. His shots went wild until at last a lucky shot shattered the broad flat head.

"I'm getting out of here!" he bawled at Jenkins who'd come running with the rest of the men. "I can't stand this cat and mouse game. I'm off!"

"You'd stand a better chance with us!"

"Oh, yeah? I don't think so. I've got

a good horse and with some water and grub I can keep riding. I want out!"

Jenkins shrugged.

"If that's the way you feel, mister, I can't stop you. At least the bastard can't be in two places at once."

Perce rode out and Joe watched at a distance. It amused him to watch the fear he was causing. It was a deadly game. Then he followed, changing horses frequently. He wasn't prepared to wear out his mounts on a little dung beetle like Perce. It was Jenkins he wanted. It was Jenkins who brought out all the Indian in him . . .

He allowed the cripple a half-day's headlong ride and more for the sake of the horse the feller rode he decided the time was right. The horse was staggering and blown and Perce beat him unmercifully and dug in his spurs to keep him going.

It was easy to outflank him and when Perce entered a deep gully which wound through a range of hills, Joe was there waiting, rifle across his horse's pommel and his second horse quietly nibbling the sparse grass.

Perce's eyes bulged. He recognized the man in front of him.

"You! The bloody white Indian! I might have guessed it. What you want with me? It's the boss you want."

"On the contrary, mister. It's you I want."

"Why? I've never seen you before in my life until we met up at the Adams's ranch," he blustered and raised his hands hurriedly as Joe shifted the rifle. "Hell, mister! You're not going to shoot me in cold blood!"

"And why not? You and that big ape you called your pard didn't give Zach Adams's brother and his wife a chance, did you?"

"But that was years ago! And anyways it weren't my idea. We was just acting on orders. What business is all that of yours?"

"It's my business because I was their son!"

"You're lying! They had no kid!"

"So Zach didn't tell you?"

"Tell us what?"

"That when he came home to his pa he found he had a nephew?"

"Yeh, he mentioned something about another heir and being cut out of his Will. Me and Rufe weren't that interested. It was Zach's business."

"Now it's yours."

"Look, mister, I want no grief . . . "

"You'll not get it. I just want you to know why you're facing the wrong end of this here rifle barrel."

"What do you want me to do? Get down and grovel? I'm not looking for trouble, mister. Just let me hightail it from here and I'll get out of this country!"

"Would you do that if you were me? Let a low-down bastard go who killed your parents?"

"I ain't had no parents! I dragged myself up. But there's been enough talk. You're bluffing. It takes a good man to kill in cold blood!"

"Then you're looking at him, buster!"

And the rifle exploded and a dark stain spread across Perce's front as he toppled slowly off his startled horse.

Joe gazed down at the lifeless body. "Meet you in Hell, dogshit!"

He turned the exhausted horse loose and covered the corpse under a mass of stones but he knew the coyotes would dig up the remains within days. He didn't care. He'd done what he set out to do.

Now it was back to face Jenkins. This time there would be no fancy games. They would come face to face. He wanted to watch Jenkins's eyes as he put the finishing bullet in him.

Then it would be all over and he could go back to Annie.

8

JOE cursed aloud. He looked down to the valley floor and watched the herd ambling along at its slow pace. But it wasn't the herd that made him curse but the men now nursing them along. And to make certain that a change had taken place he'd located the chuckwagon and it was very different to Jenkins's battered wagon.

So the change had taken place while he'd been off playing silly games with the cripple. Jenkins and his boys could be well out of the territory by now once they'd got the cash for the cows.

He pondered awhile. He certainly hadn't seen hide nor hair of them during the last two days. There was only one thing to do, ride down there and talk to the trail boss. No need to give a hint that he knew the cows were rustled.

As he neared the herd, one man cut loose and galloped towards him.

"You want something, mister?"

"You the boss of this outfit?"

"Yes, I'm Slade and trailing cows for a client. Anything wrong?"

"Nope! Just checking on a feller called Jenkins, the man delivering the herd to you."

"What about him? Seemed a level kind of guy. Didn't quibble about price and didn't even stay for a pow-wow. Took his dough and lit out."

"Where was he heading?"

Slade gave Joe a long hard look.

"Do you mind telling me why the interest in him? He owe you some dough?"

"No. I want him for other reasons which I don't aim to tell you."

"Suit yourself. But he said he was going back south. He had some unfinished business to attend to. Said it wouldn't wait."

"Did he say where?"

"Something about the Parker place

and a girl, so I reckon."

"Thanks, mister. If we meet again I owe you!"

"You're welcome!"

Joe wheeled his horse around and broke into a gallop, his second horse matching stride for stride.

Slade watched him go, relieved. The stranger wasn't hunting stolen cattle. He turned back to the herd and cracked his whip at a stubborn young bull who wanted to go his own way.

Joe was conscious of a strange sense of fear, not for himself but for the girl, Annie. He remembered the laughing brown eyes and the tender young mouth and her kindness to him when he was a wild young boy who resented white people and their ways. It had taken a lot of patience on Annie's part to gain his trust. He must have been a terrifying young animal in those first early days.

Gradually had come the change and it had hurt more than the coming of age trials of the Apache, when finally he had been forcefully taken to his grandfather, George Adams.

Now he knew that it had taken old George many months before he too could come to terms with a grandson brought up as an Indian.

But the miracle had been achieved and now Joe reckoned he was a well-balanced American and ready to fight for the Indians in any court of law. It had come to him over the years that this is what he was meant to do, to reason with white men and make them understand the Indian way of life, his beliefs and the great tribal pride whatever his nation. It was becoming clearer to him that someday, the white men and the red must learn to live with and tolerate each other.

The danger as he saw it was the threat of men like Jenkins who were ignorant and ruthless and given a little power caused the hatred and the gulf to grow wider.

The initial headlong gallop as a response to Slade's news became a slow trot, then finally a walk as he scanned the ground for telltale signs of many horsemen travelling south.

He was despairing when finally he came to a narrow stream and figuring that the bunch of riders must cross over at some point if they were to continue south, he painstakingly travelled several miles upstream before doubling on his tracks and working his way downstream.

It was a narrow ford where a wagon could cross where he found the trail and after that it was plain to be seen for Jenkins hadn't thought it necessary to hide his tracks.

But Joe was growing uneasy. They were moving into the country where Seeker-after-Truth lived. The stream was one of the tributaries that ran into the larger river. There was the possibility of an ex-army Indian scout scouting for Jenkins, reading the signs that someone was living in the vicinity. On the other hand, they might well ride on and miss the vital clues to Seeker-after-Truth's well-hidden cave.

But Joe knew the uncanny sense a well-trained scout possessed. He could smell smoke at a great distance, watch the birds ducking and diving when disturbed, sense the presence of man in that area at the base of his skull. He'd done it himself when a boy. A good scout was fine-tuned in his every sense. Joe was consumed by an impending dread.

That dread blanked out his own sense of survival. He was watching the ground and figuring just how many men now rode with Jenkins when suddenly he heard the click of a rifle being cocked and a man stepped out from behind a rock.

"Freeze, feller, until we see who you are."

Joe's hands automatically rose in the air and four more cowpunchers stepped out from their hiding places. He was surrounded. He cursed himself for being careless, but these men weren't Jenkins's men. He breathed a sigh of relief.

"I'm Joe Adams and I'm on the trail of Pete Jenkins. Know him?"

The first man nodded slowly.

"Yeh, I've heard of him. We're on the trail of stolen cattle."

"Parker cattle?"

"Yeh. How'd you guess? Or shouldn't I ask? You one of them that shot the boss?"

Suddenly all rifles were aiming at his belly.

"I was the one who got Annie Parker away."

"If you're telling the truth, where is she?"

"She's safe or she was. Look, fellers, I'm George Adams's grandson. If you shoot me, you'll have him on your tail. Jenkins is heading for the Parker ranch . . . "

"How do you know that, buster?"

"Because the man who bought your cows told me. The name's Slade. Maybe you've heard of him too? He's a regular buyer of stolen cattle and passes them on to unsuspecting buyers; need I say more?"

The rifles lowered. The trail boss looked at his men.

"He's OK, fellers. I've heard of Slade. But why should Jenkins come back into our country?"

"I figure he's after me and Annie Parker. We'd be good for ransom. I'm hoping I'm trailing behind him. Seen any movement in these parts?"

"Nope. All quiet around here but then it's a big area and we wasn't looking for men. We was looking for a telltale dustcloud."

"Then if you ride north, you'll hit the herd somewhere along the Mescalara Range. There's some big ranches over there. You might just get lucky."

"Thanks pal. What about Annie Parker? Do you want some help? I can spare one of the men."

"No. I reckon if she's done what I ordered, she'll be safe. She's holed up with a good friend of mine who'll guard her with his life."

"Good. Then we'll be off. The

foreman has a few men patrolling the ranch. They're on the lookout for trouble. You'll have to make yourself known to him or you might cop it in the back."

"Thanks for the warning. I'll watch it. Hopefully I'll be returning with Annie Parker. It's her place now. I suppose her old man is buried?"

"Yeh. It'll be a bad homecoming for her."

"Right. Then I'll be off."

The trail crew watched him go. At the top of the incline Joe looked back and waved. Then they too collected their horses and rode on.

As he came nearer to the river, Joe's foreboding grew. There was a deathless hush amongst the trees and scrub as if all the small creatures living in the undergrowth had been frightened away. It was the same with the birds. There were no squawkings overhead, but in the distance and high in the sky was a single black buzzard circling and wheeling and taking advantage of the thermal drafts upward.

Even as Joe watched it, another bird appeared and then another. Joe's jaw tightened. Somewhere down below something was either dead or dying.

He tethered the two horses in the same place he'd left them before and wasted no time in walking the riverbank to come to the place where he could climb up the side of the waterfall.

It was below the falls he found the first body with two arrows driven into the chest area. He turned it over with his boot but he didn't recognize the man.

Further on a corpse swung at a precarious angle from a tree. It too had a long expertly made arrow embedded this time in the throat. Seeker-after-Truth was an old man but he could still shoot a mean arrow. Death would have come silently and swiftly.

Then Joe, beset now by dread was scaling the elusive trail upwards and breathing hard, soon reached the cave entrance.

Inside all was ominously quiet. No dampened-down fire, no Seeker-after-Truth and no Annie. But there were signs of a fight and a blood trail led him out of the cave and up to the lookout and that was where he found the old man. He'd fought well. Two men lay near his feet like dogs at the foot of their master. Great gouges oozed blood where Seeker-after-Truth's ancient tomahawk had drunk a blood feast.

The long straggly grey hair had been tied back and he was wearing an ancient war-bonnet, so he'd seen them coming from afar and was prepared. He was also wearing a collection of lucky charms about his neck. He must have been a fearsome sight as he'd defended himself and the girl. And where was she? Had she been hiding close by or had she been already captured?

But first he must honour the old man. He could do no less. He'd given his life to help Joe and Annie. Swiftly he worked and buried him in a cleft of rock and covered the mound well with rocks. The two bodies he kicked over the edge of the small plateau and they went head over heels into the rushing waters below.

Then and only then did he look about him for signs of the girl. But she'd been there. She'd lost a shoe and a tuft of hair was snagged on a sharp splinter of rock as if she'd been dragged by the hair as she'd fought to free herself.

The bastards had got her but they hadn't brought her down the path at the side of the falls. Jenkins had been cute. He'd taken the long route, no doubt advised by the Indian scout. Men and wild animals did not leave evidence of their passing on hard rock if they were careful not to disturb small pebbles that permeated the cracks.

He checked around and found the obvious way down over the boulders. They must have carried the girl. He would pick up their trail once again on the soft ground running along the river.

He backtracked and went down the steep falls path and unloosed his horse. His own horse whinnied a greeting. With ears pricked she stood uneasily while he adjusted the saddle.

"What is it, old girl? You're mighty uneasy."

The second horse threw up its head and danced a few steps as if he too was aware of something threatening.

Joe froze. He knew the value of a horse's instinct for danger. He waited but nothing stirred. It was as if all the world listened and held its breath.

Then came the first faint sigh and then a grunt as if suppressed. It came from a jumble of rocks beyond the stand of trees and scrub where the horses were hidden.

Joe snaked forward, slowly and carefully, belly down and knife ready to hand. He was taking no chances. It could be a trap.

Then he saw him, the renegade ex-scout wedged between two massive rocks in a crevice that was destined to be his grave. His eyes flickered as he saw Joe. Then he looked down at the spreading stain on his chest. He coughed and blood oozed from his mouth.

"I'm finished. That . . . two-timing rattler . . . no dough. He . . . " He tried to take a deep breath and coughed again. "He killed . . . Charlie . . . he's got . . . the girl . . . and the cash."

"Where's he heading?" There was no response. The ex-scout's eyes closed. Joe shook him. He had no compassion for an Indian who turned his back on his own people. "Damn you! Wake up! Where's he taken the girl?"

Breath rattled in the damaged lungs and the eyes opened. He struggled to speak.

"Buffalo Spirit Canyon . . . wants . . . the . . . Parker ranch. Will marry her . . . "

"How do I find this canyon? Goddamnit! How do I find it?" He shook the Indian. More blood welled from the slack mouth.

"Follow river . . . two days, then fork west . . . follow sun . . . " And this time Joe knew he'd had all the information he would get. The man was dead. He left him for the coyotes.

9

H E was lucky. He chanced on Jenkins's trail as he travelled over soft ground. Studying it, he deduced the horse was lame. All to the good. They wouldn't be able to travel fast, especially when the horse carried two people.

Later, he came across a man's footprints. So the bastard was having to walk. The horse must be in a bad way. He forked west along a trail little used. Again he found signs of distress and then he found the bloated carcase of the horse already torn and bleeding from the buzzards.

The birds flapped heavily into the air when he approached and circled high above him. He crouched over what was left of the rotting animal. It couldn't have been dead more than twenty-four hours.

His heart lifted. With luck, the bastard wouldn't get her to the canyon. He moved on but now he was looking for signs where Jenkins might hole up. Having a woman on his hands would slow him down. He frowned. The danger was what he would do in the meantime to Annie. He thought of her smiling innocent face when she'd taught him to be a white boy again.

It all depended on her courage.

If the dogshit bastard had interfered with her or tortured her, he'd give him the full Apache works. He'd see just how much pain the sergeant from hell could take. He'd have him begging for death and it would only come when Joe was ready and it could take quite a long time before he was ready!

Carefully he tracked the meagre signs. Jenkins was being cautious and taking advantage of the hard rocky ground, but he couldn't watch Annie all of the time and Joe soon came to realize that Annie was deliberately leaving a trail whenever possible.

Once he found a ribbon, probably torn from her nether garments as she relieved herself and quietly dropped on the trail when Jenkins was busy hauling her onwards. Then he found a scrap of petticoat, caught up on a bush and, glistening in the sunlight, a hairpin. He smiled to himself. Annie wasn't panicking. She had courage.

He entered the canyon. It must be the one the ex-scout had mentioned. He looked about him and saw the rearing rock which was strangely sculptured by timeless winds into a buffalo's head.

So now he had to find the secret place which in the past, the Indians would call sacred. That would be the hiding place he sought.

His Apache upbringing gave him the answer. It would be behind and not in front of the great Buffalo Spirit.

He hobbled his horses in the shade of a rock where a muddy pool fed a patch of greenery. The horses would graze and rest.

Then looking at the great rock he

knelt and prayed, all the teachings of Grey Wolf came back to him and he shrugged off the white man's veneer. He was aware of a spiritual growth inside him, a confidence that couldn't be shaken. He knew his destiny was upon him. This was the place he would finally lay to rest all those tormenting doubts and guilts about being alive when both sets of parents were dead.

He would once and for all, rid the world of a devil man and the world would be a better place.

He stripped. At that moment he was Grey Wolf's son, Night Stalker. This was going to be the most testing time of his life. He asked Grey Wolf to bless him and give him strength. He asked a blessing from the spirits all around him, the spirits of wind and water, of the rocks and of the Buffalo Spirit himself.

He chanted the Apache war song while he daubed himself with Grey Wolf's own hieroglyphics. He bound a rag about his long flowing hair and seeing a lone eagle's feather lying on the ground, he took it as a sign that all would be well and secured it into the knot at the back of his head.

He stared at his reflection in the pool and all the western culture dropped away from him. He was as he had been brought up to be. He felt strong, with the strength of Grey Wolf and all the elements around him.

He patted both horses. They whinnied in response and then he was away at a crouching run towards the giant rock. The sun was going down and casting long shadows and he took advantage of the long blue-black splodges that changed the landscape.

Nothing stirred and yet he was confident that out there were two people and soon, one of them would have to show himself.

Then he made a decision. The white part of him was impatient. He wanted to face this man and get it all over. He looked about him. Where was the best place to reveal himself?

Then it came to him. The Buffalo Spirit Rock was in the middle of a natural arena. Where better than stand facing the rock and on the highest tier of ground?

It was like climbing a giant staircase. Then he was standing with legs apart and arms outstretched. He looked an impressive sight with hair blowing in the wind, his painted chest and bare feet and only his trousers to cover him. He looked wild. He was wild and above all, he was wild inside.

The Apache warcry reverberated around the canyon, echoing with sinister insistence. There came a puff of smoke and then the sound of a shot. Joe was conscious of an angry bee buzzing past his head. He yelled in exultation. Nothing could hurt him. He was charmed, a nemesis, come to extract his revenge.

He'd noted from where the shot had come. Crouching low, he scrambled and slid down to the canyon floor and then made for the rock.

Several blind shots were fired as if in panic. He had no weapon other than his knife, so there was no answering fire. This had to be an Apache execution in honour of Grey Wolf and Blue Cloud.

He climbed the lower slopes of the big rock and soon found a faint unused path where many feet had trod in the time before the white man.

He knew there would be many paths upwards to join together to come to the sacred place. He wondered which path Jenkins had taken.

Then as he was tackling an overhanging rock he heard the scream. It was coming from above and to the right of him. He swung himself clear of the overhang and lying on his belly, he watched the drama ahead, helpless to aid Annie who was trying to scramble down the rough path with Jenkins close behind.

"Come back, you fool!" he was shouting. "You'll go over the edge and break your neck. Do you want that?"

"Get away from me!" She slipped

and slid a few more feet.

"Annie! Make you way over here!" Joe called.

Annie looked around, hearing the voice but because of the overhang she couldn't see where the voice was coming from. "Annie! It's Joe. Climb to your left, Annie, to your left!" She made a desperate effort to reach the protecting overhang.

Pete Jenkins's gun blazed in warning.

"Annie, come back! I don't want to shoot you." He watched helplessly while she scrambled farther away. "You little bitch! I've a good mind to . . . " He broke off his threat as Joe appeared above the overhang and his reaction was to shoot, snapping off slugs until the gun was empty. He cursed.

Joe laughed and it echoed around the canyon walls, amplified and sinister.

"I'm coming for you when I'm ready, Pete Jenkins. Take a good look at me. I'm your nemesis!"

"Aw, go to hell where you belong, you white trash! I'll be ready when you come! You don't think you can frighten me?"

"We'll soon see, won't we? But for now you can clean and polish your weapon in good old military style and be ready, for you won't know when I'm going to strike!"

"You're a crazy man! You've got the girl. Isn't that enough for you? Or are you after the dough for the cows? It's hidden well, buster. You'll never find it!"

Joe ignored the taunt. He was too busy helping Annie over the last rough ground and literally lifted her on to the ledge of rock where he now stood.

He drew her trembling body into the protection of the overhang. Her long hair was wild and tangled, her body glistening with sweat and the rents in her gown revealed scratched and bruised skin.

He held her close, smoothing the hair from her eyes. She stood, panting with eyes closed, her body tense. Gradually he felt her relax.

"Don't be afraid. You're safe with me. I'm the boy you tamed. Remember?"

She looked up at him with a tremulous smile.

"I remember. I remember every little bit about you. I missed you terribly when you went away."

"Well, I'm here for you now. Has that bastard hurt you in any way? I mean has he . . . ?"

She flushed and hung her head.

"No. He said he was going to marry me and he didn't want any complications. If I accepted him he would leave me alone. I said I would marry him . . . he's not interested in me. He wants the ranch now that Pa . . . is gone." She tried to suppress a sob. He held her close.

"I'm sorry about that. Major Parker was a good and fair man, not like his sergeant. Annie, you've got to trust me. I've got to leave you for a time. You must stay here. There's no food or water. Do you think you can last out?"

186

She shook the hair from her eyes and looked up at him.

"Jenkins fed me and I'm not thirsty but how long will you be?"

"Not long, but it could be overnight and perhaps most of tomorrow. Can you manage that?"

"Yes, if I know you're coming back."

"I'll come back. I promise you."

"You're going to kill him, aren't you?"

"Yes. I've no choice in the matter. You remember how I was when I came to you? All beaten up and your father said he took me to save my life?"

"Yes, I remember."

"Well, Jenkins didn't only do that to me but he raped my Indian mother before he killed her. I can't let him go now."

"And I wouldn't want you to. Don't worry about me. I'll wait and I won't wander off as I did when I was with Seeker-after-Truth. They wouldn't have found us if it hadn't been for me. I feel dreadful

187

about the old man. He was very kind."

"What's done is done. It was the old man's time to die. He would be prepared, believe me."

Annie looked at him oddly.

"You really are Indian, aren't you?"

"In essence, but in all other ways I'm Joe Adams, grandson of George Adams and hopefully his heir when this is all over. Now I'll be away, and you pray for me, Annie. I can use all the help I can get!"

He kissed her, at first tentatively, expecting her to slap him but she didn't and his hold on her tightened and the kiss deepened until she was kissing him back.

He broke away from her, stirred with blood pounding. He would have liked nothing better than to stay with her through all the night hours. But his vengeance was stronger. He must finish what had to be done and then the slate would be clean and he could start a new life and leave the old one behind.

"Annie, I must go . . . "

"I know."

"When I come back . . . "

"Yes, Joe?"

"Never mind. Trust me. I'll be back," and he sprang for the edge of the rock and disappeared upwards. She felt her fingers on her lips. He'd kissed her as if he really meant it!

She felt a new strength within her. She could endure anything, heat, sun, thirst and hunger as long as she knew he was coming back to her.

But what if Jenkins proved a more skilful opponent than Joe expected? After all, Jenkins was a seasoned campaigner. Joe was too young to have been a warrior back in his Apache days. Maybe Joe was taking too much on his shoulders. What if he didn't come back?

The thought panicked her and she found herself praying as she'd never done before. Oh, God, please look after him. I've nobody else . . . please send him back and I'll never have a

189

bad thought again . . .

Joe moved silently and quietly and gradually gained the back of the huge rock. He'd guessed correctly for there was a huge crack — where once frost and ice had broken the giant crag and water had seeped down over thousands of years and caused a tunnel which was smooth and dry and choked with dust. It led into a larger cavern and there he found the trappings of ancient rites and ceremonies and the far newer signs of recent occupation.

But there was now no sign of Jenkins or any of his gear. He must be fully loaded up and he would be slow in climbing and unless he could move on the hard rock he would leave deep footprints.

But now night was falling. In two hours he would be unable to see any tracks. He would have to track him on instinct and sound.

This would be where he scored. He'd been trained by Grey Wolf to track in the dark, whereas Jenkins would be helpless. It would be like a blind man seeking a man in the dark. He would have all the advantages.

He found a trickle of water and bathed his head and drank, then followed the trickle of water and found it led upwards. He sniffed the air. It should have been dank and foetid in the ancient tunnel. It was not so there must be another outlet.

Soon, the tunnel narrowed and dripped water. Somewhere ahead there must be a spring of some kind. Maybe the source of water for the ancient shamans who lived in the Buffalo Spirit Rock.

Then he stepped out into fresh air and found himself on the very peak of the rock. It was a lookout. If it had not been dusk he could have seen right along the canyon from one end to the other.

Then he saw the fire, a wink of light in the distance. For all his boasts Jenkins was up and running. It looked like a small enclosed fire, perhaps just enough to boil coffee but being so far above it made it possible to see the flickering flames.

He must get down and off the rock. The hunt was on and, taking note of the direction of the fire by studying the first of the night's stars to show, he made his move and, like a shadow, slid and scrambled his way down to the floor of the canyon below.

Then breaking into the wardog's steady trot and imagining the steady pounding rhythm of a wardrum inside his head, he adjusted his running and settled for a long hard jog.

He lost sight of the fire when he descended the great rock. No matter, he had the stars to guide him. He ran on, adjusting his breathing to a comfortable machine-like motion.

The moon came up, blue-washing everything in its eerie light. He reckoned it was time to take care and move like a mountain cat after its prey.

He sniffed smoke and tobacco long before he saw the small camp and

Jenkins huddled against a rock, his head nodding but one hand grasping his rifle. As Joe watched, he saw the head come up, look around and then drop as if the man was exhausted.

Joe smiled to himself. The bastard had run until he dropped. He was a loud-mouthed bag of wind, a bully who needed others around him to prop him up. Now, he was on his own and he was shit-scared.

Joe crept nearer, confident that Jenkins's untuned ears would not pick up any sound. He scooped up a dollop of hard clay and hefted it in his hand. This would set his guts working if nothing else!

He waited until Jenkins sat comfortable, his head on chest and then he threw the ball of clay. The impact of the clay against rock was loud in the still night. Jenkins jerked upright, showered in small powdery lumps. Joe could hear him curse.

"What the hell . . . !" and then he was on his feet looking about him. His rifle rattled at his feet forgotten as he grabbed for his handgun. He fired three shots in a panic in different directions. "Who's out there? Damn you, show your face!"

But Joe moved silently to another position and watched Jenkins examining the ground and finding nothing but freshly broken clay. He removed his hat and mopped his brow and then sat down again laying both handgun and rifle close to hand.

Three shots gone, Joe mused. He wondered just how much ammunition Jenkins carried. It would be amusing to find out. He settled himself to wait. The moon was sailing quietly across a clear sky. It was a giant orb and easy to calculate the passing of time.

Again he threw his missile when Jenkins relaxed but this time sent two in quick succession. Jenkins jumped to his feet and screamed into the night.

"Damn you! If you're out there, show your face! Stop playing games! I know it's you, Night Stalker! You miserable white Indian who's neither one thing or another! Come out and fight like a man not a bloody snake!"

The answer was the distant growl of a jaguar on the hunt. Jenkins stiffened and Joe smiled as he watched the fear in him. Joe thanked his father for teaching him the sounds of everything around him. The scream of the puma, the mating call of the caribou, the cry of the jack-rabbits and the calls of the birds. All had been a means to an end when they were out hunting, especially at night. The teachings came back to Joe in an overwhelming sense of acute loss. It was as if Grey Wolf stood beside him and was speaking in his ear.

"Take it gently, my son. Whatever the prey, he will react in the same way. He will know he is being stalked but as he cannot see you, his imagination will play him tricks. His fear will kill him in the end, whether it be man or beast."

So all he had to do was have patience.

He watched Jenkins in a detached

kind of way. At that moment he could have killed him with one throw of his knife. But the memory of Blue Cloud and his own torment at the hands of the man made it impossible. The ex-sergeant had a lot to answer for.

Slowly the man dropped to his knees and Joe heard him sobbing. Then Joe took a deep breath and out came a sigh like that of a wind in the trees. Then came the whisper.

"You remember me, Sergeant Jenkins? I'm Blue Cloud . . . you remember, don't you? Blue Cloud . . . Blue Cloud . . . " The whisper died away.

It seemed to be in the air and all around him. He crouched low on the ground and closed his ears with his fists.

Joe heard him moan. Then he watched as his body thrashed in a fit, his limbs shaking grotesquely. Joe came nearer and watched. It was interesting to see how fear would take a man.

It was then he took the bullets out of the rifle and handgun and searched about for extra shells. He found a small cache in his jacket pocket. Jenkins hadn't planned his last exploit with much finesse. He found the bulging payroll for the stolen cattle and reasoning that it belonged to Annie, took it. Then stealing away, he cached it and waited.

It was coming up dawn when Jenkins was strong enough to crawl to his fire and blow up the embers to a blaze and then fed it with sticks he'd collected earlier. Then he brewed up the remains of last night's coffee.

Meanwhile, Joe had inched his way around the rocks and was now squatting about twelve feet above him, a lump of clay in his hand. When the coffeepot bubbled and the aroma of coffee steamed up to him, Joe struck. The clay knocked over the pot and the coffee sizzled amongst the wood and the fire went out.

Jenkins cursed and looked upwards. His eyes bulged when he saw Joe crouching directly above him. He grabbed his handgun while Joe poised to jump. He grinned.

"Go on, shoot! You've not got one goddamn bullet for either weapon. Go on, please me. Try it!" Jenkins in desperation pulled the trigger several times. Then as Joe sprang into the air, he flung away the gun and turned to run.

But he was weak and slow. Joe landed on his back but the force of his landing sent him off and away from Jenkins. It gave the man a chance to turn and face him. He lashed out with his hands and feet and then Joe had him by the throat and they kicked and rolled and clawed each other and brought blood and once Joe was conscious of the heat of the embers as they rolled back and forth all over the ground.

Then Joe felt the man beneath him stiffen and then flop and he knew it was all over. The evil eyes, still the eyes of a killer, fluttered open.

"Kill me and have done."

"You think it will be that easy?"

The eyes widened in shock. Joe laughed and his lips drew back from his teeth like that of a jaguar, or so the fevered mind of Jenkins saw it.

"You're a white man. You'll make it quick."

"That's the first time you've ever acknowledged I'm white. Why shouldn't I treat you as an Apache?"

Jenkins swallowed.

"I'm going to die anyway. Just get on with it!"

"Right! But first we must think of Blue Cloud. You raped her before you throttled her, so as I can't rape you, I'll do this instead!" and his knife bit through Jenkins's trousers and blood gushed from the clumsy castration.

Jenkins screamed.

"Then this is for Annie," and he slit the scalp and tore off what remaining hair Jenkins had.

He dangled the bloody trophy before the man's eyes.

"You don't tangle with an Apache's

womenfolk and not pay for it." Jenkins's mouth was open but no sound came. Only the eyes were alive and knew what was happening.

"And this is for me." The broad Bowie knife sliced through Jenkins's heart and the hatred died out of the bulging black eyes.

Joe drew back, covered in the man's blood. He collapsed beside him, more from the mental strain than the physical. Then, collecting the payroll in its leather bag, he trotted back to the river to wash and to give thanks to the spirits before returning to Annie.

The sun was high overhead when he finally climbed up to the hidden overhang to where Annie waited.

She saw his shadow before she saw him and was waiting when he finally came to her. She searched his face anxiously as he looked grim and somehow years older.

"You all right? You're not hurt?"

"Not physically hurt."

"You mean . . . ?"

"I came face to face with myself and I didn't like what I saw. I can't explain it. My heart was as black as Jenkins's."

"What about him? What happened?"

"He's dead. I tried to make it an execution and I failed. I enjoyed what I did and it was wrong."

"But he was a bad man!"

"Yes. I suppose it makes me very human after all. Anyhow, enough about me. Were you frightened?"

"Frightened for you, not for me. I thought you might not come back."

"Doubter!" He lifted her chin with his finger. "I told you to trust me," and he kissed her lightly on the mouth.

She relaxed into him and they stood for several precious moments while they savoured each other's bodily warmth. Then she shivered.

"I'm hungry."

"I'll take you back to the sacred cavern and then I'll go hunting. If you look about you might find something to cover you. You look a bit of a mess!"

He grinned at her evident distress. "Oh, don't worry. I love you as you are and always will!"

"Joe . . . ?"

"Yes?"

"I love you too and I always will!"

"And so you should. We were made for each other. Now come on, the sooner we get to the cavern the sooner I find us something to eat."

Later, they sat before a blazing fire and Annie watched Joe cook jackrabbit, Indian-style and they drank cool crystal-clear spring water and it tasted like nectar.

She had found Jenkins's bedroll and they sat together absorbing the comforting heat. Then he sighed and putting an arm about her, kissed her hair.

"Tomorrow we must go back. Tonight, well, we have tonight," and Annie snuggled closer.

* * *

George Adams, leaning on his cane, stood on his veranda, shading his eyes with his hand. He watched the two horses and riders coming at a slow walk.

He'd kept this vigil for many days. He'd never given up hope that his grandson was out there somewhere. His only fear had been that Joe might revert to his earlier life once again in the wilderness. He had never quite believed that he had his grandson back for good.

He'd taken the news of Zach's death in his stride. For him, his son had been dead for many years. As for the woman, Tilly, she probably deserved what she got. He could never abide loose women and she'd looked as loose as any woman of that ilk.

There was something about the riders that was different. His heart gave a flip leaving him dizzy. Could it be . . . ? He bellowed for the Mexican housekeeper who came running.

"What is it, Mister Adams? Are you ill?"

He stretched out a shaking hand.

"Look out there. What do you see? Is it . . . is that my grandson's horse with him aboard?"

The fat old woman shaded her eyes and searched the arid landscape.

"I see two riders . . . "

"Yes, yes, you old fool! But the one riding the bay! I'm nearly sure!"

"It could be, Mister Adams. Should I call one of the men?"

"Yes. Get someone to saddle my horse. I'm going out there to meet them."

"But are you well enough for that, sir? You've been peaky these last few days."

"Never mind that, woman! Just give me a horse!"

George Adams hadn't been aboard a horse for some time. It was an effort but he gritted his teeth. No one could say an Adams couldn't do whatever he made his mind up to do. He'd done what he wanted all his life. Now if it was his grandson coming back, he wanted to be out there to meet him. There was a gladness in him tinged with worry. What if . . . ? He could hardly bring himself to admit how much he wanted the boy back and settled and the hint of wild restlessness gone forever.

He loved that boy. There was an honesty in him that had not been present in either of his sons. He was too old not to face facts. If Joe decided the wild free life was for him, no amount of bribery would keep him by his side.

He rode slowly not because of his infirmity but because he would know by the boy's face whether this was a fleeting visit or whether Joe was coming home. There was a woman with him and she looked like an Indian, wrapped in a blanket and her long black hair flowing wild. His heart sank. He couldn't compete against a lifetime of freedom and the imbibing of the Apache culture and the boy was bringing a squaw home to prove it.

His face was stern and his voice cold

when finally they came within speaking distance. He was startled at the change in Joe. He'd gone away a boy. He'd come back a man.

"So you're back. Was it tough?" His eyes swept the girl briefly.

"Sort of."

"It was Zach, wasn't it, who started it?"

"Yes." The old man nodded.

"He and the woman are buried together. I'm sorry, boy. I shouldn't call you boy, should I?"

Joe's lips curled a little in a tired smile.

"No. I'm a killer. Can we move on? Annie is at the end of her tether."

"Annie?" Old George gave her a hard keen look and saw the fatigue, the utter physical breakdown held together by willpower. He saw something else. He recognized her under the dirt and squalor. "Good God! It's Annie Parker! We thought you were dead!"

Annie lifted her head briefly and tried to smile.

"Not yet. Joe saved me." Her eyes closed and her head flopped like a broken blossom.

"Hell! Let's get her to the ranch!"

"That's what I'm aiming to do, Grandpa!" The sarcasm was wasted on the old man. Joe tightened his hold on Annie's leading rein and kick-started his own mount and they made their way back to the ranch.

Word had got about and the punchers working the home ground were there to meet them. Eager hands drew Annie off her horse and carried her gently into the house, where Carmen the housekeeper took over.

Joe endured some back-slapping and a barrage of questions and heard the news of the return of the Parker cattle. Then, dropping the bag containing the rustlers' proceeds on the kitchen table with a brief, "This lot belongs to Annie", he went off to bathe and change.

★ ★ ★

Later, when the lamps were lit and Carmen had served the two men their meal, she came back beaming.

"The *señorita* is awake and hungry. She will be fine after a good night's rest, thank the good God!"

Old George went to the redwood tallboy and opened it up and produced a bottle.

"This calls for a special drink. I've kept this bottle for such an occasion as this. We might as well break it open."

Silently they drank together. Both knew that the drink wasn't only because of Annie, but because Joe himself had come back safe. Then finally Joe spoke in the dark with only the glow of the fire.

"Grandfather, we must talk."

Old George sighed.

"I know what you're going to say. You're leaving me and going back to the wilderness."

"No, Grandfather, you've got it wrong. I'm not going back. Out there,

I laid my ghosts to rest."

"You mean you're not leaving me?" Relief made him dizzy or maybe it was the strong liquor.

"No. Ever since I was old enough to know what happened to my natural parents and to my beloved Indian parents I've lived with a sense of guilt that I didn't do something about it. Out there, I came face to face with my past. I was given the chance to clear up past debts. I killed Jenkins. It was inevitable. He was the one responsible for all the hate yeasting inside of me. As for my own parents . . . the two men who killed them are dead and Zach, who was their boss is dead. I didn't kill him, Grandfather but I would have done if I'd had the chance!"

The old man nodded, head bowed.

"I'm glad you didn't, Joe. It's not good to spill family blood. It poisons the brain and affects your thinking ever afterwards. You're haunted for life . . . but he had to die, Joe. He was born bad and broke his mother's heart. But no more of that. Will you go back to San Francisco?"

"No, Grandfather. I never liked city life. I only stayed because you wanted someone in charge of the office. They can manage quite well without me. You've got some good men looking after the freight and stagecoach business."

"Then what do you propose to do?"

"I'm marrying Annie and helping to run the Parker ranch. It's all arranged. Last night . . . "

He stopped abruptly and old George's wise old eyes softened.

"Ah, now I see! It's the girl who's tamed you?"

"Yeah. She did from the very start."

"Then I'm pleased. I might even be around to see my great-grandson!"

Joe laughed but didn't answer as the door opened and Annie put her head around the door.

"May I come in for a minute?"

Joe's breath caught in his throat. This

was a beautiful Annie, hair washed and shiny and twisted upwards in a knot. The white cotton nightgown was far too big but it was covered by a giant colourful shawl she held closely about her.

She smiled at Joe's reaction but it was the love in her eyes that broke down the last barriers. Oblivious to his grandfather, he strode over to the door and swung her up in his arms.

"You shouldn't be out of bed," he whispered.

"I couldn't go to sleep without seeing you. You look all right."

"Yes, and better still for seeing you."

"Have you told your grandfather . . . ?"

"Yes, and he's pleased. He's already talking about great-grandchildren."

She blushed. "Joe, kiss me and then I'll go back to bed."

"I'll kiss you, but I'll carry you back. You're too frail and delicate to move around much!"

Her laughter rang out loud and clear as she hugged him close.

"How dare you say that? After all I've been through!" She turned to old George. "Believe me, sir, I'm a very tough woman! I'm not one of your namby-pamby ladies, and I call a spade a spade!"

"I'm sure you are and do, and don't call me sir! I'm your grandfather now, for God's sake! Welcome into the family!"

THE END

FIGHTING RAMROD
Charles N. Heckelmann

Most men would have cut their losses, but Frazer counted the bullets in his guns and said he'd soak the range in blood before he'd give up another inch of what was his.

LONE GUN
Eric Allen

Smoke Blackbird had been away too long. The Lequires had seized the Blackbird farm, forcing the Indians and settlers off, and no one seemed willing to fight! He had to fight alone.

THE THIRD RIDER
Barry Cord

Mel Rawlins wasn't going to let anything stand in his way. His father was murdered, his two brothers gone. Now Mel rode for vengeance.

ARIZONA DRIFTERS
W. C. Tuttle

When drifting Dutton and Lonnie Steelman decide to become partners they find that they have a common enemy in the formidable Thurston brothers.

TOMBSTONE
Matt Braun

Wells Fargo paid Luke Starbuck to outgun the silver-thieving stagecoach gang at Tombstone. Before long Luke can see the only thing bearing fruit in this eldorado will be the gallows tree.

HIGH BORDER RIDERS
Lee Floren

Buckshot McKee and Tortilla Joe cut the trail of a border tough who was running Mexican beef into Texas. They stopped the smuggler in his tracks.

BRETT RANDALL, GAMBLER
E. B. Mann

Larry Day had the choice of running away from the law or of assuming a dead man's place. No matter what he decided he was bound to end up dead.

THE GUNSHARP
William R. Cox

The Eggerleys weren't very smart. They trained their sights on Will Carney and Arizona's biggest blood bath began.

THE DEPUTY OF SAN RIANO
Lawrence A. Keating and
Al. P. Nelson

When a man fell dead from his horse, Ed Grant was spotted riding away from the scene. The deputy sheriff rode out after him and came up against everything from gunfire to dynamite.

FARGO: MASSACRE RIVER
John Benteen

The ambushers up ahead had now blocked the road. Fargo's convoy was a jumble, a perfect target for the insurgents' weapons!

SUNDANCE: DEATH IN THE LAVA
John Benteen

The Modoc's captured the wagon train and its cargo of gold. But now the halfbreed they called Sundance was going after it . . .

HARSH RECKONING
Phil Ketchum

Five years of keeping himself alive in a brutal prison had made Brand tough and careless about who he gunned down . . .

FARGO: PANAMA GOLD
John Benteen

With foreign money behind him, Buckner was going to destroy the Panama Canal before it could be completed. Fargo's job was to stop Buckner.

FARGO:
THE SHARPSHOOTERS
John Benteen

The Canfield clan, thirty strong were raising hell in Texas. Fargo was tough enough to hold his own against the whole clan.

PISTOL LAW
Paul Evan Lehman

Lance Jones came back to Mustang for just one thing — revenge! Revenge on the people who had him thrown in jail.